Call Me
Marigold

WATTLETALES
PUBLISHING

Lindy Warrell

WATTLETALES
PUBLISHING

Published by Wattletales Publishing
Adelaide, Australia
www.wattletales.com.au

First published by Wattletales Publishing in 2026.

Wattletales Publishing and the author acknowledge that this book was written on the
lands of the Kaurna people, traditional owners of the Adelaide Plains.
We pay respect to Kaurna Elders, past, present and emerging.

Cover Design and Typesetting: Nicola Matthews, Elect Printing, Canberra.
Printed and bound in Australia.

ISBN: 978-0-6453129-7-3 (Paperback)

Cataloguing-in-Publication entry available
from the National Library of Australia
https://catalogue.nla.gov.au

Marigold begins her story with her fictional death and retraces her life, both good and bad. It is a stained-glass window of emotion, and a prism of golden sovereigns that yields to the subdued blue of a calm ocean. Her eucalypt and ochre outback experiences with our First Nations' people are a joy to read. The dark, leaden outlines surrounding the whole represent injustice and sadness, so be prepared to feel outrage.

Yet, *Call Me Marigold* offers a fascinating portrait of a life pulsating with honesty and contradiction. It is vulnerable yet tough, loving yet wise, and the throughline of Marigold's conversations with her mother is a touch of brilliance.

Just to peek through the glass is a privilege.

Veronnica Cookson

I dedicate this book to my three children,
who suffered my ignorance as a mother for far too long,
yet became beautiful human beings.

a
posthumous
tale

of
unforgotten
moments

Prologue

I was born weighing eleven pounds on February 11, 1943, and died after eighty-one years on earth on Sunday, December 8, 2024. Baby stories about me are about how heavy I was, how hot it was, how complicated the gestation and birth were for my mother and what a letdown my father was to her.

Throughout my childhood, people asked what I was going to be when I grew up, as though I were nothing then. Now, I am without a future. I can neither check the Bureau of Meteorology app on my iPhone nor watch the news on the telly to help me decide what to wear. Not that it matters, I am intangible, with no need of clothing, and any sense of shame died with me. All that remains of me are thoughts. Perhaps that's all I ever was, a collection of unforgotten moments.

I call myself Marigold so I can revisit embarrassing incidents and secrets without betraying myself or harming others. It may seem somewhat contrived, even for a pen name, until I tell you that the marigold represents so many things around the world, from joy and resilience to death. And, as I discovered after the name popped into my mind, in Buddhism, the marigold signifies a journey toward wisdom and compassion. I am not sure I ever got that far, but we shall see as my story unfolds. For now, I am floating in limbo, unable to rest, until I understand my life.

A few years before I died, I paid for my funeral—nothing flash. I asked to be laid out in a wicker coffin swathed in white cotton with my lifeless face naked of makeup. And, by the cultural logic inherited from my parents, not unlike circumcising a baby boy because doctors cut his father, I specified cremation, with my ashes to be spread at sea. At the time, I didn't realise that leaving funeral instructions was a risk; it doomed my wishes to be eternally unrequited.

Christmas

Let me take you back to a day about a month before I died. I was sitting on my tiny balcony, shedding soft yet painful tears, as I frequently did in my old age, when above the humdrum of traffic, joyous wafts of childhood reached out to dry my eyes. The Glenelg Christmas Pageant was wending its way down Jetty Road. You see, I lived my last years in Manson Towers in Glenelg, an eight-storey, independent living retirement village, a hundred or so metres from Jetty Road, the beach and, on that day, the pageant. Before that, I led a peripatetic life both as a child and an adult. At one stage, a few years ago, I calculated that, on average, I'd moved every eighteen months throughout my life.

My Christmases were just as diverse. I don't remember much of the very early years, but in Japan, where I'll soon take you, Christmas was a lavish Western affair in post-World War II Tokyo.

As a publican's daughter, I spent most of my early Christmases in pubs around Australia. My family moved a lot. I cooked turkey and British-style Christmas roasts for family and customers on a black cast-iron wood stove in Oodnadatta, a town of approximately a hundred permanent residents. Despite its distance from all that mattered, in that pub we hosted a wide range of visitors, dignitaries, priests and chaplains, politicians, salespeople, and tourists, as well as servicing the surrounding pastoral properties. To pastoralists, their ringers and staff, we were their local.

Temperature control on an iron stove fired with mulga stumps was an art. A standard fan stood in the corner, wafting over our large, green-painted timber kitchen table and work benches more to keep the flies away than anything else. Sadly, when Dad eventually bought us a gas stove and installed air conditioners in the bar and our family bedrooms, the kitchen missed out. We loved the warmth of the fuel range in winter, but in summer, the fan was useless. We hit 47° C once.

Regardless of which pub we lived in as a licensee family, every year, Mum, Dad, my little brother, and I had to serve a full Christmas dinner to the kitchen, bar, and wait staff once the guests left. Mum hated Christmas. It was a lot of work, from ordering supplies to designing a menu and accommodating sometimes demanding customers. I inherited a similar disinterest in the red-and-green snow traditions we Australians inherited from the Northern Hemisphere.

Before my second marriage collapsed, my husband, children, and I were lucky not to have to fight with in-laws about who would go to which family on Christmas Day. My husband's family were Dutch migrants, and fortunately, they celebrated Christmas Eve as the primary event. In those years, our festive meals were still largely traditional British fare. After their father left, the kids, my parents, brother, and I had our Christmas lunch at a local Chinese restaurant. We all enjoyed Chinese food and the chance to select what we fancied.

Once my children left home, I moved hither and yon around Australia, often spending Christmas alone or joining in the occasional orphans' Christmas dinner with other folk who either had no family or whose loved ones lived abroad or far away. The first time I ate that celebratory meal alone after divorce and the loss of both of my parents, I took myself to a nice hotel where the wait staff hovered over me as though I was a lost kitten. I spent many birthdays on my own, too. For my seventieth, I treated myself to a fancy hotel lunch. I mentioned to the friendly waitress that it was my birthday, and she asked how old I was. When I finished my main course, she and another waitress surprised me with a delicious sponge cake, dripping with syrup, and a serving of ice cream topped with sparklers, singing Happy Birthday, and everyone in that busy dining room joined in as though they were family. How special was that?

I also spent my father's last two Christmases in the dining room at the War Veterans' Home, where he spent his last days.

Christmas is a Bugger

Dad and his cronies
bob their heads over bibs
in tune to carols
at the War Veterans' Home
as nurses dance around wheelchairs
serving food, pills and kisses
in red and white-bobbled Santa caps.

The larrikin lost in the war
rises through glazed eyes
as faint memory
flickers in cheeky grins
and faces brighten over ill-fitting
mothballed best clothes.

Military issue cigarettes
are nowadays banned and dad's
being weaned off Mogadon
by a new matron who warns
it'll kill you.

'Silly bloody woman,' he'd say.

In my later years, my daughter and I would get together most years. She cooked a roast, which we would have with roast potatoes, salads, cherries, and ice cream. My youngest son joined us from Brisbane when he could. We adapted our food preferences to the Australian weather, and treated Christmas as a secular occasion to give thanks and connect with family when we could. My eldest son lived abroad from the age of eighteen.

Mum, I wonder if you or Dad ever worried about dragging me all around the country as a child, from state to state, town to town and pub to pub. It took me aback to learn from a documentary that frequent moves for children were abusive. The show was about Circus kids deprived of outside friends and a community beyond their family. Unlike me, those kids didn't even go to school; they were home-schooled. Although I didn't have any long-lasting friendships either, I'd say our peripatetic years (which I kept handy as a habit of escape) did me no real harm. Similar to circus kids, we just had a different community of family, staff and guests. It is true, though, that even after I left the pub-life circus, it was never easy for me to maintain long-term friendships.

Strange and contradictory things resulted from my upbringing. On the one hand, I became competent and independent. On the other hand, I was emotionally introverted. The mix made me brash. I developed a capacity for quick wit and smart answers, and even as I grew older, my acerbic tongue was ready to protect me. People often said I scared them, even when I didn't speak to them that way.

Manson Towers

I spent nine happy yet declining years at Manson Towers, my retirement village in Glenelg. For many of us who lived through the 1960s, the name Manson was a daily reminder of the notorious American murderer, Charles Manson. Manson Towers was built in 1972 of yellow bricks, then in fashion. Less spectacularly, the building was named after a person I'd never heard of, one Mr PG Manson.

Like much of Glenelg, this nine-storey block of independent living units emerged from the demolition of a stately mansion built by an early colonial resident. Premier Don Dunstan officially opened Manson Towers in 1973. Glenelg has since grown as a tourist destination where elderly residents and local and international visitors alike have access to colourful events, music, markets, shopping, restaurants and a tram service on the doorstep to and from the city, not to speak of a long jetty, a Norfolk Island Pine-lined esplanade for promenading, and a white-sandy beach.

History aside, I loved my little balcony overlooking a deciduous tree-lined car park behind the Esplanade's Ramada

Grand Hotel, a perfect spot to see, hear, and feel the world go by. Opposite me was the rear entrance to the recently renamed Colley Hotel (built in 1869), freshly painted white with black lettering. Next to that, facing my unit, was the beige side wall of a heritage-listed building that had been a backpacker hostel for many years. After the hostel closed, the building stood empty for a long time before becoming a foreign-student hostel. Shortly before I died, another new owner listed the building for demolition to make way for a new nine-storey hotel to be built behind its 1878 heritage-listed façade. I didn't get to see that.

However, I did oversee the emergence of a new, seven-storey luxury hotel, The George, from my little balcony. It sprang up from a jackhammered site on the far side of Jetty Road, parallel to Manson Towers. After weeks of jackhammering and excavation racket, two giant cranes magicked themselves into the sky, one blue and one orange. I became dizzy watching the hi-vis-clad operators climb up and down their crane's zigzagging stairwell to the operational pod many times a day. Such things got me pondering the complexities of lives and worlds I know nothing about.

No matter how pretty or fascinating Glenelg was, folded around the shores of Holdfast Bay, inner-city living brought a ghastly screech of power brakes and the companion thrum of idling engines from delivery trucks and garbage disposal units, filling my days and starting outside my unit as early as 3 am. By necessity and practice, I overcame my distaste for these ugly sounds by giving thanks that our city was clean and that people had somewhere to mingle and enjoy life in their spare time, eat well at one of the many restaurants and ice-cream shops in this seaside suburb, or fall in love in the sun. I am sad that I missed the grand opening of The George by a whisker. It was not far from opening when my time was up, but living where I did had me thinking how odd it was for me, who grew up in pubs, to die surrounded by them.

Given my initial intense animosity towards South Australia, I never understood why I returned to spend my final years there. Still, I did, only to fall in love with the whole state, from outback deserts to the inner city. Adelaide gave me so much: children, a tertiary education, travel, and friendships through poetry and writing, which brought joy and satisfaction to my old age. One thing I learnt along the way is that you never know where life will take you, but it always reveals who you are if you dare to face the truth.

Mum, you could never understand why I hated South Australia, wanting to escape as I did for many years. At first, it was pettiness on my part. You robbed me of an exciting future just as I left school and was about to start my first job at ICI (whatever that stood for) in Melbourne city, and you said we had to move because of my baby brother's health. If you recall, Dad sat in on my first job interview, which people in recent times may think ridiculous, but at fifteen, it made me incredibly proud.

Do you remember when we first arrived in Adelaide, there was a heatwave that made me loathe the scorching, dry heat after being surrounded in Melbourne by gracious, tree-lined streets that I loved. Do you remember sending me out of the house to collect acorns from St Kilda's streets as a little girl to feed zoo elephants (as you told me), which, looking back, was probably a ruse to get me out of your hair on busy days. Also, looking back, I see now that being forced out of my happy place when Japan had already been hard, but moving far away from Melbourne put another dent in my innocence. I resented the dry South Australian heatwaves, especially as you grizzled to me for years that you had given birth to me, an eleven-pound baby in a stinking Melbourne heatwave, as though it was somehow my fault.

WWII and Palestine

In the year before I died, Russia's Vladimir Putin kept bombing his way towards possessing Ukraine. In Israel, under Benjamin Netanyahu, a sky full of Israeli bombs razed Palestine. Social media and protests denounced Israeli atrocities, and many declared Netanyahu to be a war criminal. Too old to protest in the streets about such brutality, as millions around the world were doing, I cried at television portrayals and made modest donations after seeing Palestine's children almost wiped out as the likelihood of peace receded beyond the horizon.

Televised images of Palestine's devastation triggered my childhood memories of Hiroshima after America's atomic bombs hit it and Nagasaki, killing hundreds of thousands of civilians at the end of World War II. Mum and I saw the devastation of Hiroshima from a train window two years after that shocking event. We had recently arrived in Japan to join Dad after a long sea journey. In horrified innocence, we gazed at shattered, urban buildings standing like hollow ghosts in a grey-white landscape of rubble and ashes stretching to the horizon, where family homes and flourishing green fields had thrived.

I had ringworm. Mum put a protective arm around me as though to shield me from the deathly vista while she daubed me with Gentian Violet-soaked cotton wool to ease the itch. I was purple all over for days. We didn't speak. There were no words for what we had seen. Those images echoed in me all my life. The only street march I ever participated in was an anti-war march. I remember also arguing with my Honours supervisor over a group dinner. He argued against abortion and was pro-war in exigent circumstances. My view was the complete reverse.

I don't remember where we were going on that train, probably Tokyo, where Dad was stationed. He had arrived in Japan months earlier as part of the British and Commonwealth Occupation Forces (BCOF). He always claimed we should thank the Americans for winning the Second World War, yet all these years later, I still want to ask him why the atom bomb was necessary when that war was effectively over. What might he have thought about Donald Trump, whose Presidential madness made the world tremble?

I felt that Trump's second presidency would mark the end of a beautiful restart after WWII, one that flowered in the words of a war baby like me, Bob Dylan, who brought hope to the world with his powerful lyrics, *The Times They Are A-Changin'*. And change they did for the better.

Our war baby cohort soon gave way to the baby boomers (1946-1964), a sizable postwar generation born to women who worked while their men served in uniform far away. When the war ended, the female workforce was demobilised into domesticity to make way for returning men, the breadwinners, as they used to say. Ironically, in this context, one of the most significant changes brought by the boomers twenty-odd years later was a powerful and persistent feminist revival. So, just as my life seems to have been staged, beginning and end, with a hotel setting, war provided the historical bookmarks of my existence.

Do you remember, Mum, travelling with me as a little girl on those Chinese sister ships chartered by the British Admiralty as supply ships during WWII? The Taiping on the way, and the Changte on return. Those names imprinted themselves on my mind. Remember playing quoits and table tennis on deck. I loved those games. They even had a swimming pool, such a luxury, although I was terrified of King Neptune with his trident when he baptised us in a flurry of splashing with his retinue for crossing the Equator. He still looms huge in my aged mind, albeit as a shadow rather than a being.

My Parents

My father was born in 1910 in Glebe, New South Wales, then a Sydney slum. He used to tramp three miles back and forth to school barefoot and became a bookie's runner at six. At fourteen, he joined the navy and later worked as a hotel dishwasher at the Victoria Palace Hotel on Little Collins Street in Melbourne, where he soon rose to become head waiter. It was there that he met Mum, born in 1919, who was an apprentice hairdresser in a shop opposite the hotel.

They met around a piano at a party where Dad, already engaged to be married, was singing to surrounding admirers. At that time, Mum had a boyfriend who had a motorcycle, whom she mentioned on and off all her life. My father also had a motorbike. He had a flashy sidecar, which he'd fill with flowers while waiting outside for Mum to finish work. He was flamboyant, as they used to say. My mother, in contrast, came from an impoverished family, fallen from Melbourne's elite. Looking back, I now see why I always considered bawdy Sydney as Australia's father city and Melbourne its genteel lady.

Whether Dad wore military khaki and shiny boots or danced in striped pyjamas with me as a little girl on his feet, singing light opera in his tenor voice like Mario Lanza's, he was a happy soul. Not so my mother, who acted posh and proud. I used to wonder if that was a cover for her family's decline, a feeling compounded by her commoner husband's unabashed joy in life.

Surprisingly for a publican, Dad was a teetotaller who controlled others through charm and feigned friendliness. Mum was an introvert who nevertheless spoke her mind without regard to others' opinions, which was unusual for a woman who explicitly raised me to pay attention to what others might think of me.

Over the years, I came to understand that Dad's bonhomie was his mask. He buried his yearnings in gambling. Mum was a critical person, hyper-critical, some might say. She pushed people away and escaped into the booze.

Although my parents hated each other's weaknesses, they were fiercely loyal to each other in the face of the world, and that protected me. My childhood was, in some ways, like living in a dangerous whirlpool of noxious emotions, but they were steadfast in their love for me. Still, there were times when one or the other would turn on me to relieve frustration. 'Your mother always was jealous of you.' Dad would say to curry favour. And Mum insisted I was emotionally cold, 'Just like your father', when she was angry at him. Or, drunk.

My parents never hit or abused me, not even yelling. Ironically, my mother's way of chastising me or showing her disapproval was to remain frigidly silent and refuse eye contact. She withdrew her love cruelly at times, which made me terribly anxious until she allowed me back in her good graces. Even in old age, I was always extremely uncomfortable with conflict, especially when it involved someone I cared about. I hated being ghosted online, too.

Although Dad didn't chastise, he was demanding and expressed disapproval and disappointment if, for example, I didn't do what he asked, such as looking after my younger brother. His lifelong belief was that, as a girl, I should look after his family; my mum when she was drunk and my brother, when it got too hard. These things to him were not part of a man's role.

My parents died when I was in my fifties. They were always involved in my life. Ours was a tight-knit family, as were many at the time, until the bonds that held us became socially unacceptable after being redefined psychologically as co-dependency. That notion bothered me because my parents anchored me even as we, and I, moved around. They were my place, my home. (I should have written an article about the breakdown of the village, tribe and extended families to create the individualised monad—each person a capitalist consumer—but I left it too late.)

As part of Aussie history, Mum's family was of the fallen gentry; Dad's was early convict stock. That's the Australian social order I grew up with right there. I missed Mum most after she died, and you'll hear from her as we go. She remained my life muse, a resident voice in my head. For now, it's enough to know that Mum and Dad were as different from each other as button-up boots are from slums.

Japan

While much of my childhood was lost to the winds of time, occasionally, faded images of innocence floated around me like pieces of frayed or tattered cloth, as did my memories of early childhood in Japan, a valuable part of me.

Before he died, my father bequeathed me his collection of bleak, wartime-grey photos of Japan. After years of barely suppressed jealousy, my brother appropriated them. Born when I was ten, he had not shared my Japanese experience, but as a son, he believed he had a right to his father's military history. One of the photos I managed to keep was of the hotel where my parents and I lived.

Like all our wartime photos, taken mainly by the military, the Marunouchi Hotel photo showed a sturdy yet grey and dejected nine-storey building, a perfect reflection of the times. In the last year of my life, a friend who travelled to Tokyo took photos of the hotel for me after a 2007 rebuild. The transformation was miraculous; the Marunouchi had additional glittering storeys and a totally different façade, yet still stood proudly on what I assumed was the same site.

In similar grey tones, a photo of my bedroom in Marunouchi showed a single bed with a chenille bedspread and one pillow, a bedside table with a wind-up alarm clock with two bells, a book, and a teddy bear on top. Years later, my own children's rooms were similarly spartan compared to the fluffy, overloaded affairs in which little ones were growing up several generations later.

I wrote the following sketch about the Marunouchi when I planned to write a novel set during the occupation, titled *Beyond Ginza*. I was going to use a child narrator to reflect on my life as an army brat.

I used to hide in a small but frequently used function room in the Marunouchi Hotel when it was closed to khaki, buckles, boots, and the flotilla of silk, taffeta, and velvet-clad wives, who floated red, white, and blue like a rainbow to the tune of alcohol fumes passing from glass to lipsticked mouths.

Despite boot-bruised arcs and pitting left by spiked heels, I could see my face reflected on the parquetry dance floor, shone by Japanese hands. I felt both safe and comforted by the soft black-and-white patter of the uniformed staff outside the room as they went about their business in the morning, when the hotel awakened. I wasn't sure if they knew how often I slept there. I did know from the softening of their faces as I passed them on the way back to my parents' quarters that they pitied me, a little seven-year-old girl in a strange land whose mother plaited her hair too tight when she was drunk and whose father was a genial gambler who—and I might be making this up—had started to slide to the dark side.

At another time, in Nikko, I was sulking on a hilly lawn below

Call Me Marigold

Nikko's golf course clubhouse, where officers and their wives mingled and drank and flirted across nations. Not wanting anyone to see how angry I was, I plopped down on the lawn, poked my head between my knees with arms wrapped around them, after my mother told me to play with an Indian Embassy diplomat's little boy. She wasn't thinking of me. She didn't even ask. She wanted to impress, even though I'd heard her and Dad laugh when the Americans mocked Indians for not using toilet paper and being arrogant. I wanted to scream and stamp my feet, but dared not go that far.

Instead, I willed a little ball of orange-coated chocolate to roll my way from the Jaffa packet beside me. I took my eyes off it for a moment to take a sneaky look back at the clubhouse where the Indian boy was still standing on the veranda in a white frilly-fronted buttoned coat and baggy cotton trousers. I didn't notice the Jaffa roll down the hill; I was so busy giggling, thinking the boy had to stand upright to keep his turban in place. His skin was dark, close to black, quite striking, really. The way he stared into the distance from beneath long lashes with indecipherably large brown eyes intrigued me. I was curious to know whether he considered himself superior to me, as I did to him.

Hunger gnawed at me. No, I was starving. I frowned and pursed my lips to maintain my anger as I snuck another look at the veranda. I wanted Mum to ask me up for lunch or Dad to tell her she should, but she was too busy drinking and flirting, and he was sidling up to the big brass. Dad was fun at home, dancing in his pyjamas. It made Mum jealous.

Our weekender in Nikko had tatami mats and movable rice-paper screens for walls and windows. They were perfect for punching holes in to let everyone know how I felt, but I was never game to give that a go. Anyway, the frames quietened the house and filtered daylight in a uniquely calming way. There was a cook somewhere, and we all sat on the floor at a low Japanese table for meals. Everyone praised me for being the first in our family to use chopsticks properly. When visitors came, I roamed in the woods, and one day, one of the servants introduced me to her grandmother, an old woman she told me to call Mamasan. Mamasan spoilt me with mounds of freshly steamed rice piled into a dainty bowl with soya sauce and tasty bites. The rice aroma calmed many aches in my heart, and I loved steamed rice forever.

After lunch one day, Mamasan took me to a rock pool in a grove at the bottom of the hill; its water was so clear that you could see your toenails underwater. There, I played with some Japanese boys around my age. I wore togs (swimming suit or bathers), but they were unselfconsciously naked as they vied with each other to make the biggest splash when jumping off the rocks into the cool water. They were as shy with me as I was with the Indian boy, but friendly, always smiling and including me. I climbed on the rocks and jumped with them all afternoon; nobody at the house missed me.

It was hard to go back to the weekender after such freedom; I never knew what awaited. One day, Mum and her visitors were playing Chinese Checkers. When they asked me to join them, I felt all grown up, but I lost. The adults drunkenly laughed out loud. I cringed at that mocking sound before the most enormous fury overtook me. I swiped the board and checkers off the table and ran into the night. Nobody came after me. I finally crawled into bed just before dawn, trying to get warm.

Back in Tokyo, I eventually succumbed to life as it was in the Marunouchi. Best of all, my mother took me on outings around the city and beyond. Her young, handsome Japanese chauffeur made me laugh and feel special, so I grew jealous when she paid him too much attention, fluttering her eyelashes and lowering her gaze. Still, she was fun to be with when she was sober and left her pretensions behind. Wanting to please this version of my mother, I vowed to be nice to the Indian boy next time we were in Nikko. To please her. I never forgot his beautiful, shining brown eyes.

Mum, I didn't know how to tell you and Dad how miserable I was, so far away from home. Not in Nikko, where I met Mamasan, who caressed my face and head with kindness as though I was special. I mean, in the hotel. I hated having a Japanese nanny in my bathroom. When she attempted to wash me, I put on a pretend tantrum and threw the soap at her, splashing and yelling until she bowed backwards out of the bathroom, looking terrified, poor woman. As I look back now, I didn't hate her; I put on an act because you weren't bathing me. I wanted you, and you left me with the staff so often while you talked to important people. As for Dad, I couldn't even try to explain; he would never listen to my side of any story and always said, 'You're only a little girl, what would you know?' Only. I hated that word. Sure, I was an only child, and at that time, it was a statement of fact, but being 'only a little girl' turned me into nothing. That's how it felt.

Mum in High Society

The Daphne Story

Tokyo. Post World War II,
Occupied Japan to be precise.
The Australian Army sent
my father, a Major, to co-opt and manage
The Marunouchi Hotel
for British Commonwealth forces.

My mother soon joined him there.
In a cheap fox fur,
jaws clasped to bushy tail on her breast,
she wore a saucy black hat,
lace veiled her eyes,
masking her innocence.

Before long she succumbed to mink,
a full-length coat, seductively plush
beneath which silk lining there lodged
a leaden heart and forgotten smile
that had turned to gin for courage.

It was at a dinner for Red Robbie—
Lieutenant General Sir H.C.H. Robertson of course —
that mother succumbed to
her wilder side, her spirited side, her red lips
pouting beside the Occupation Commander himself.

That night well drunk
from talking and laughing and wanting
to smash through uniforms and decorum
my mother ate daphne from Red Robbie's table.
She destroyed his delicate centrepiece.

Military rank thus exposed as weak left guests stupefied,
too frightened to speak, but the General
burst out laughing. So, the guests exhaled and returned to
smoking and drinking, and lots more flirting,
passing foreign time in a soporific cloud of arousal.

Mum, I sincerely hope you don't mind my using The Daphne Story to talk about your drinking. I often worried about what you were thinking at that Japanese dinner party with high-level officials and their pretentious wives. Were you embarrassed for eating the daphne? It's one thing, isn't it, for me to talk about what I recall from family chatter, and another to know what your experience was. At a guess, I'd say you were mortified, but from what I do know, you were not one to apologise. Instead, you'd go cold and lock your feelings deep inside. If you could tell me now, would you say you were only twenty-four, desperately unhappy in your marriage and out of your depth with the bigwigs you had to entertain? Is that when alcohol first became your friend?

I didn't notice it too much as a small child, but later, in my teen years, it hit me hard because you became someone else when you were drunk, saying hurtful things about me in front of people with deep resentment, like, 'You're as cold as your father,' as though I had ruined your life. Do you remember that, when I was older, I would collect you from the toilet where you'd passed out with your undies at your ankles, to put you to bed? You ignored the fact that Dad made me your carer when you were like that. Only towards the end of my life did I begin to understand how sad and lonely you must have been in your marriage, but all I can do now is tell you that I died loving you more than you could ever know.

Dad No Longer a Major

At the end of World War II, Dad left the army, where he'd
served well, with the distinction of being promoted to the
rank of major. Sadly, as my brother and I discovered when
our father died aged eighty-seven, his elevated rank was a
temporary promotion for the duration of his assignment
in Japan, a position he gained solely on the basis of his
hospitality experience. The army would not allow us to put
'major' on his headstone. It broke our hearts. When Dad
returned to civilian life at home, he was a successful hotel
manager whose publican's licence was unblemished. I often
wondered whether he knew.

As a man, my father was a riddle of unpredictable moods.
Charming and funny in public, but surly and often angry at
home; generous when he won at the races, but when he was
broke, he joshed his way out of saying anything meaningful.
He was fun to be with most of the time. When we returned
to Australia, we lived in a large, rented room in an old
mansion-turned-boarding house on Redan Street, St Kilda
in Melbourne, where we sat cross-legged for meals around

our carved Japanese dining table, in the same room where we slept. That was the last time my parents slept in a double bed, except once many years later. I had a truckle bed on the other side of the room. Those were happy years. Dad would lovingly joke that we were mummy frog, daddy frog, and baby frog, and we'd laugh together. Later, in most of the pubs where we lived, our private, family space consisted of two single beds in one double room for my parents and a single bed in a separate single room for me, not always on the same floor or in the same corridor.

Back then, sweet delights consisted of a Violet Crumble or a Cherry Ripe from my maternal grandmother's overcoat, if I guessed the right pocket. Ironically, Nan had diabetes and couldn't eat such things herself, but I remember her boiling her urine in a little pot on a green enamel gas stove every morning and adding a chemical reagent to see if it had changed colour. Violet Crumbles were the oldest Australian sweet treat, first introduced by Hoadley's in 1913. The Cherry Ripe, produced by MacRobertson's Chocolate, was introduced in 1924.

I was lucky. My generation had the freedom to explore. The streets were safer (fewer vehicles), and we could stay out as long as we were home before dark. Those were the days of Clydesdale horses pulling bread carts, and delivering ice for ice boxes, milk in small metal cans left at the gate and bags of coal for heating. Cream was inches deep atop the milk. There was room for self-generated creativity.

For the most part, in my memory, when Mum was soporific on booze, Dad became maudlin in ways I couldn't understand. Despite often being confused by such experiences, I was safe and felt loved in those early childhood years. My parents were always there. Finding Mum arranging fresh flowers next to the reception desk or in the entrance foyers of various larger hotels we lived in, delighted me. Her face would brighten ever-so-fleetingly in response to my unguarded rush of love when I found her after school. When Dad joined us in those moments, his belly laugh of joy, gratitude, and wonder sealed us as a family unit. Nights, however, were often dark.

I remember one morning when I was about nine years old, opening the door to my parents' room (we didn't lock our doors then) after hearing loud choking sounds within. I found Dad sitting on the floor, his head between his knees. When I asked what the matter was, he first said 'nothing', then mumbled that he didn't think he could bear it anymore before turning to me, wiping his eyes and forcing a smile. 'Don't worry, little one,' he said. 'It's a grown-up thing.'

Years later, I learnt from my favourite paternal aunt (the sister Dad disliked the most) that she had taken Mum to Melbourne around that time to have an abortion, but Mum's pregnancy was too far advanced. She had wasted time taking hot baths and drinking hot gin to rid herself of an unwanted pregnancy. My brother was born several months later. Despite rumours that he was the offspring of a Dutch head waiter in the New Albury Hotel, when my brother grew up, there was no mistaking that he was our father's child. He looked like me, like Dad. The staff had concocted a rumour to hurt my parents. Yet, my parents' deep loyalty to each other kept them together for over fifty years, despite their proclaimed mutual antipathy.

Mum and Dad were an unlikely couple. Dad had no education beyond early primary school, and even though Mum's mother was born into a family where staff used to fasten her button-up boots, she had no formal education either. When Nan married a commoner, her family disowned her. After giving Nana three little girls, Nan's falling-down drunk husband died by hitting his head on a mantelpiece. Nan had no work skills and soon lived on a few bob a week from cleaning rich people's homes in and around St Kilda. My mother didn't want to marry; she wanted to be a doctor, but ended up working in a factory because attending university was beyond her mother's means. Nan raised her three girls alone.

Over the years, my parents confided in me, in snippets, their disappointments and dissatisfaction. Dad maintained that Mum's drinking created the rift between them. Mum convinced herself she drank because her husband cruelly denied her sex. While they both loved me to bits, they were jealous of each other's love for me, which, if you think about it, gave me bargaining power. Still, I was piggy in the middle, and it hurt me to see them hurt each other.

School and Friends

It's incredible how things going on around you trigger you. Sometimes it might be something someone said, or the taste of ice cream that opens a zip in your mind. One day in my eighties, I was eating a bowl of Connoisseur Salty Caramel Ice Cream, chuckling, guilt-free of the watch-your-weight mob, when my mind turned to childhood, when there was no such thing as a self-serve fridge full of individually wrapped ice confections in shops and petrol stations. Instead, small, local deli owners sold square ice blocks in square cones. Choices were few—vanilla or raspberry, and milk or water. I can't recall any other variations. Those icy treats quickly turned the cones sticky and soggy, but we sucked on them without leaving a skerrick of flavour behind. After school, we sometimes frequented what was then the only milk bar in Albury, New South Wales, for a milkshake. My favourite flavour was blue heaven, a vanilla-raspberry blend tinted blue with food colouring.

Until I was ten, I wanted to be a pianist or ballet dancer. All the good girls played the piano, proudly showing off that they were off to practice in a display of superiority. All I could think was that their parents were wealthy enough to pay for tuition and buy a piano, not to mention a house big enough to accommodate it. Most of those girls were brunettes with brown eyes. They were also teachers' pets and snobs who were mean to the likes of me, living in a pub.

On Not Being Me

Long fingers and slender calves,
oh! How I wished that were me.
I was never fussed about my button nose
because I didn't know much about those,
but looking back,
it matched fat hands and thick thighs.

Redheads' freckles
made me glad to be blonde
with blue eyes, yet I yearned
to have the seriousness of shiny dark hair
like the clever girls, first in class.
I took comfort in the back row—
being a smart arse.

Teachers' disdain for me
trickled down the pecking order
to protect the dark-haired, clever girls
who pinched my lunch
and let down my bicycle tyres
while I hid in the toilet, scared and alone
wishing I wasn't me.

Call Me Marigold

At the New Albury Hotel in Albury, where these tales belong, there was a piano in the ladies' lounge adjacent to the formal dining room, where tables stood to attention with starched white tablecloths and serviettes shaped like a pope's mitre. The ladies loved our handsome pianist, in a black tailcoat, stiff-fronted white shirt, and bow tie, even on bright, hot summer days, as he played a popular mix of Chopin classics or relaxing tunes every afternoon and during all meals except breakfast.

It was hard for me, between the ages of ten and twelve, to practice the scales in that environment, but I plucked up the courage to give it a go once or twice when the pianist took a rest. Those hardcore tipsy ladies mocked me until my face burned red. I then turned to ballet and practised assiduously in my room. During classes, I'd stand on tiptoe, pretending to be *en pointe*, arms reaching above my head, hands posed in what felt like a graceful movement that pleased my girlish heart. The teacher said my legs were too fat. It didn't matter whether I could have learned to dance; I was out.

Because I was an avid reader and proficient in English literature and grammar (taught as two distinct subjects at the time), elocution followed. Although my parents sent me to those classes to improve me, as it were, I took to it with glee because I loved words. I learnt poetry and how to throw my voice and speak well. We used to learn poems by heart, long poems like T.S. Eliot's The Love Song of J. Alfred Prufrock and Samuel Taylor Coleridge's The Rime of the Ancient Mariner, reciting them while walking in circles, a book on our heads. The motto was that good posture leads to good diction, and both were useful for young ladies. The mood was very much of the June-Dally Watkins era, who, I believe, was the first to introduce a finishing school in Sydney in 1950, where girls would become young ladies through elocution, etiquette, and deportment classes.

School was a whole other story because I was so often the new girl, moving as we frequently did to accommodate my father's restless soul. Even late in life, when I read the word 'inkwell', I could hear the sound of chalk screeching on the blackboard after class as I wrote one hundred lines intended to somatise the idea that I was worthless: 'I am a bad girl and promise to respect my teacher'. I could not even pee until I'd finished. It didn't seem to matter that a teacher might smell like cigarettes and Scotch whiskey. They hated me, assuming I was terrible because my parents were in the hotel game. Parents similarly feared that I would contaminate their daughters if they played with me. Those homes were off limits.

My first friend in Albury was J, and by contemporary standards, the things we did as pre-teens may seem ridiculous, but my strongest memories were of immense freedom and the joy of being with her. I remember us riding on the centreline of wide, empty streets in the shade of giant Plane trees in Albury, standing on the pedals, pushing for speed, then flopping back onto the seat to kick our legs out as we freewheeled from the effort, screaming—poo, bugger, bum—and laughing so hard our tummies ached, convinced that our words would fly higher than a kite. Such a long time ago. Such naivete. We had yet to learn what would happen to us when we became women as defined by puberty. Thank goodness we got to yell and scream modest obscenities and giggle with no repercussions, at least for a short time.

My parents liked J. They used to admonish us with a smile to beware of tramps when we went bush on our bicycles. We never bumped into a tramp, but the warning brought a frisson of fear to our adventures. I never worked out whether my parents meant to scare us or were genuinely worried about tramps, having lived through the Great Depression, when homeless men walked this vast land seeking work.

We rode on country roads as free as birds, looking for an appealing stand of gums inside a farmer's fence that told us a creek would be nearby. We only ever found dry creek beds, but we'd lie down beneath the grey-green swoop of eucalypt leaves at its banks with arms behind our heads, our eyes following dappled white clouds race across the sky through the canopy. We had our quiet moments, reflecting, dreaming, and listening to the bush on still days, its whispering air, rustling leaves and grasses, bird song, crows cawing, insects buzzing and maybe a baa or a moo in the distance until one or the other of us would speak, breaking the spell.

When we chatted, we had a lot of questions about Aborigines. Schools taught us about white explorers, with no mention of them. Aboriginal people in our conscious world were like mythical creatures, as though the actual tribes had vanished from this land, which satisfied the then-prevailing orthodoxy that Australia was discovered (sic) *terra nullius*. At that age, we were more curious about personal things, such as whether they wiped themselves with leaves after toileting. Our First Nations traditions, cultures, and histories failed to engage the national consciousness for decades.

After a while, J began worrying that her parents might find

out about our exploratory rides far from town. Her father was a working man, somewhat unkempt and unwashed. He wore a white singlet that showed wiry black shoulder hair and curls that clung like a dank fringe to his chest. His wife was a strict soul, a Christian homebody who cooked the best Golden Syrup pudding in the world. I loved going to their place for Sunday lunches with J's older sister and grandmother. We all squeezed around a small kitchen table, which made it cosy and so different from eating alone in a pub kitchen or dressing up for a formal dining room meal, where I had to be quiet so as not to upset guests.

One day, the mood in J's house changed. Her parents had learnt that mine were publicans. They said they were sorry, but I couldn't come to their place again. Once word got out, I felt like an outcast at school, where nobody would play with me, until R and I became friends.

R's father was a railway worker, and her mum was a free-thinking schoolteacher. They didn't care that I lived in a hotel or that Mum was a drunk and my father a habitual gambler. R's house had a new-fangled, tub-styled washing machine with wringers to squeeze excess water from linen and clothes, and her father was one of the first in town to own a car. It had a dickie seat. They included me in all sorts of family outings, such as picnics by the Murray River and Bonfire Night for Guy Fawkes' Day on November the fifth. Each year, they built a massive bonfire in their backyard, and when darkness fell, they lit fireworks that exploded like gunfire and coloured the sky while we children ran around with sparklers. Those were amazing times that taught me what makes a happy family.

R and I reached puberty together. We were really too naive to realise what that meant, but she had an older brother whom I adored. He was a tall, athletic, freckle-faced, red-headed flirt. I used to get all *thingy* when he was around (I had no words for such feelings back then). Guilt sometimes had me wondering whether I hankered after R's friendship to see her brother.

R's family was great, and their house was always full of laughter. Although, or perhaps because, they had enough money to buy a car, we had to share bathwater. (Water was reused in the washing machine, too.) The bathroom precedence was that R's older brother bathed first, then her little brother, and then we two girls had to sit in the boys' grey water and soap scum together. Being immersed in the water that had embraced R's older brother's body tickled my yearnings, something I could never share with R, but her mother never missed a trick. One thing I did learn at R's place was the anguish of blushing. I swear, the woman had eyes in the back of her head.

I'm glad that my family left Albury before R's mother banished me from her house, too. I did not, for a moment, miss the taunting I'd suffered at school when I unwrapped my chef-made sandwiches at lunchtime, from a starched white napkin. I so desperately wanted to have brown-paper-bag lunches like the other girls. I yearned to fit in.

I doubt you thought anything about my friendlessness at school, Mum, and I was too ashamed to tell you about that. But do you remember how you taught me good manners with the words, 'What will other people think?' With that, I grew up so other-oriented that, by the time I was fifteen, I vowed to become a nun and retreat into the arms of God, whom Protestant Nuns had—as I later learnt—dishonestly taught me never to judge. You may not have known this either, but that escape wish, and my early bulimia both swiftly vanished when my seventeen-year-old navy cousin kissed me on the back veranda of our Caulfield rental in Melbourne as I was just about to begin my working life. That kiss changed my course even more than our new black-and-white television set. What fun, I thought. Boys.

Buddha Memories

One day, a friend's partner joined his wife and me for Uber lunch at my place. He commented on my ornamental Buddhas. In a small retirement unit, as he pointed out, they took on the quality of a collection. I'd never seen them in that light before, any more than I'd thought about my three ex-husbands as a collection. Nevertheless, his words resonated, so I decided with a wicked grin to offer stories of my six Buddhas as a collector might, one object at a time, as I will later with my three husbands and three divorces. After all, this is a disposition of memories, not a historical record.

I accumulated eight Buddhas over the years. However, by the time I moved into my retirement village with the mass murderer's name, only six remained. I donated a large brass sitting Buddha from my post-retirement years as a meditation teacher to a Cambodian Buddhist monk who was my friend. It found a home in his temple on the other side of town. The transparent resin Buddha gifted to me by the head monk of Adelaide's Sri Lankan Buddhist Temple found its new home with my youngest son.

The first Buddha statue I ever bought came from Sydney's Chinatown near Paddy's Markets, where I worked after the first of my three failed marriages ended when I was barely eighteen. I got a job with a company called Pardy Providors as a stenographer and cord-and-plug telephone exchange operator. My boss was a tall, well-statured man who wore brown suits and constantly hitched his trousers at the crotch. In my late teens, I had to suppress the urge to giggle at this unfortunate habit. Still, I never mocked, as he was a kindly soul who took care of me when I once had a telephone flirtation on the exchange with a supply officer from the Ingleburn Army Camp, a purpose-built training centre during World War II, which wound down in the mid-1990s. I don't recall his name, but we flirted whenever he called to place an order. He finally persuaded me to meet him, but my darling boss saved me. The guy was married with two little ones.

Had I met my telephone paramour, I might have suggested meeting at The Broadway Hotel on George Street, where I worked a second job at night as a barmaid. Being a publican's daughter had its benefits: I could always find a pub job for extra money, or when other options were scarce. In Sydney, I first lived with my aunt—my father's least favourite sister— in North Ryde, which was then one of the city's semi-rural outposts. We had an outhouse and a dunny can man who collected the waste on Friday nights. Much as I loved my aunt, I didn't like going outside to the loo, especially not on wet winter nights. Also, travelling to and from work each day meant long walks, plus trains and trams both ways. So, I got a second job and moved into a boarding house on the curve of Bondi Beach, right next to its saltwater pool.

I didn't purchase my Chinatown Buddha until after my second disastrous marriage, on a trip to Sydney for my first academic conference years later. By then, I was an impoverished, single-parent student in my forties. The place where I bought it reminded me of Pardy Providors, but the timing of the purchase carried the pain of being deserted by my second husband, who was my children's father. The statue was a rotund Chinese laughing Buddha in a blue porcelain robe, with six happy infants crawling over his bare shoulders, a profound symbol of love and joy, all hope of which I lost when my second marriage failed. That Buddha remained one of my favourites till the end. It survived many house moves along the way.

Twenty years later, when I was in my sixties and living in Melbourne, I bought a sixty-centimetre-tall, gold-resin standing Buddha, laughing with outstretched hands, each holding a ball aloft, a travelling Buddha representing prosperity, happiness, and good luck. I found it one day while wandering lost at Melbourne's Victoria Markets, looking for my car on the wrong side of that vast, sprawling marketplace. Its gold lacquer glinted in the sun from the window of a shop, drawing me in when I was exhausted. I found the darkness inside calming. The elderly Chinese shopkeeper dressed in what I guessed was traditional rural Chinese garb—loose trousers and a top made of rough hemp or cotton—greeted me with a smile. 'You like?' he asked. 'I'll give it to you for a special price—you are my first customer. That is my good luck.' It was good luck for me, too, at a time when I was feeling utterly drained by life, after being shafted by my erstwhile workplace.

I had been working for the NT Government on a joint Commonwealth and Territory-funded project to lay an ethical foundation for obtaining consent from First Nations people to store their health records electronically. I had an office within an Aboriginal Medical Services Alliance surgery, one of many participating surgeries in the trial. I played a small part in developing culturally appropriate consent guidelines with the National Health and Medical Research Council.

Being sandwiched between three levels of governance was, to say the least, problematic. At one meeting, my ethical concerns about data storage plans were dismissed by some and mocked by others. Soon after, I left the project and moved to Melbourne, my birth city, where two of my three children lived.

When I first arrived, I put my name down for public housing and within a few months, was offered a bedsit in one of Melbourne's tower blocks right in the heart of Prahran, a place I adored, close to St Kilda, where I was born. After a year or so, I returned to Adelaide, a place I once hated, but had grown familiar with, where I could buy a small house, rather than a bedsit or tiny flat in the outer suburbs of Melbourne. My gold Buddha's luck served me well in my transition from anthropology and the workforce to retirement in South Australia, filled with meditation, poetry and writing.

I concede that the purchase of two of the remaining Buddhas had an aesthetic impulse. One is a small figurine carved from Sri Lanka's shiny black ebony, which I purchased for 900 Sri Lankan rupees from a Colombo jewellery shop in the 1980s. It holds memories of the country I lived in and loved, where I met my third husband. Another statue is a gold-and-white porcelain Chinese meditating Buddha, bought from the Nan Hai Pu Tuo Temple in Sellick's Beach, near Aldinga Beach, where I had my little house. It entered my life when I began to write in retirement.

Another Buddha in my so-called collection was a traditional Sinhalese Sitting Buddha in resin, about forty centimetres high. It was a gift many years after I left that country from the man who was my PhD research field assistant, who told me he had it specially crafted by a traditional artisan. My assistant went on to become an international consultant of some note, and we remained lifelong, long-distance friends. In our old age, we still emailed a few times each year to stay in touch. His wife died not long before me, and my heart broke for him.

When I moved into Manson Towers, I scoured the internet for a small Daibutsu Buddha, a replica of the thirteen-metre-high bronze statue in Kamakura, Japan, where I first fell in love with the figure as a child in post-war Japan. I was thrilled to find a tiny, sixty-millimetre bronze replica that was cool to the touch yet weighty to hold. As I died, I clasped that little Buddha in my palm.

Speaking of friends, Mum, try as I might, I cannot remember you having any friends, and Dad certainly didn't. He played golf with acquaintances, mostly returning customers, wherever we happened to be living. I can recall two women you called friends. One, in Albury, was a wealthy customer who was a drunk and your drinking companion. In South Australia, a well-to-do pastoralist's wife was your favourite drinking buddy. It hurt me that she invited you to her house when she felt like having a weekend binge. I later learned that she and one of her daughters, who became my friend, always thought we were beneath them. We were a pair, you and I, weren't we? Only in old age did I experience care from people with no expectations. I hope they know how much I appreciated that.

My Brother

My Brother

I miss you, my brother
like no other
we were friends
you and I.
Mother feared
for you,
your health and growth
but I held
your flights of fantasy
an insanity
that broke your heart
so gentle and kind
till you fizzled into stardust
that nothing could contain.

My brother was just under ten years my junior. He was born in 1952 in Albury, New South Wales, where Mum and Dad managed the New Albury Hotel. I yearned to hold him as a baby, love him, and take him for walks when he grew. I wanted to play with him, but our mother always kept us apart because a doctor told her that a ten-year-old girl would be jealous of her new male sibling and might harm him. We both grew up encoded with that imbecilic medical sexism, and we played it out many times in our younger years.

Soon after we moved to Oodnadatta, my parents sent my prepubescent brother south to board at Rostrevor College, a Catholic school. Why? I blamed the rough chauvinism of the bush. Ringers and pastoralists alike mocked and teased him for being what they called a pansy, as though they had an animal instinct telling them that he was gay before he understood that word himself. He was desperately unhappy at Rostrevor yet fell in love with Catholicism, and at eight years of age, he wrote to the Pope asking to be christened into the Church after the school refused his requests, saying he was in love with the pomp and pageantry. They may have been right. Nevertheless, the Vatican issued instructions that he be Christened forthwith as a Catholic, and he was.

As an aside, my parents had the Americans christen me in Japan as Episcopalian (Anglican). Mum was Protestant, and my father, a Catholic who carried small catechisms and prayer cards from childhood. When Dad died, I found them nestled deep in his socks and handkerchief drawer.

Not until Mum and Dad took my brother out of Rostrevor in his early teens to attend Norwood High did he tell me who he was. Back then, the term 'gay' in Australia had not yet gained legitimacy; it was still barely a whisper from overseas. I was driving him home after school when he was about sixteen, and he shared his precious secret with me. He told me that he didn't fit in with the other boys because they talked about boobs and girls, and he wasn't interested. He was an intelligent, sensitive and arty boy with no interest in football either. Many years later, he received a substantial legal settlement from Rostrevor College for the appalling treatment he endured there.

Looking back, my brother was emerging into the gay social scene in Adelaide at a fragile age for any boy, at a time when gay bashing was a familiar gutter sport, until three men, including Doctor George Duncan, were brutally murdered and dumped into the River Torrens. Many described those deaths as a watershed moment for what were then known as queer rights. Homosexuality remained illegal in South Australia until three years later, when an openly gay Premier, Don Dunstan, decriminalised it: a first in Australia.

Nearly forty years later, on December 9 2017, Australia legalised gay marriage. I wept, wondering what my darling brother would have thought.

I adored ballet as a pre-teen, and loved ballroom dancing and jiving at nightclubs. All that stopped when I had children and responsibilities, but my love of dance had me fixed to the screen when Dancing with the Stars began. When my brother was sixteen, I took him to see a ballet classic—I can no longer remember which one—in a town hall in Elizabeth, South Australia, of all places. I think it was the only time I ever went there. He fell in love with dance too and, before long, joined the Australian Ballet School, later dancing with the Australian Ballet Company in Melbourne.

He also danced in Europe and elsewhere for some time but came home, wrecked. I can still see the pain on my parents' faces when he stepped from the plane at Adelaide airport, dishevelled, skinny and wild-eyed. With their fearful support, he soon recovered and was accepted to study classics at the University of Adelaide, where I was already studying.

Over the years, my brother and I became very close. We shared everything. No secret was too unsavoury to mention. We fought at times, of course, and things went pear-shaped occasionally, but we vowed as sober, clear-minded and open-hearted adults that we were and always would be the good guys to and for each other.

He died aged fifty-two.

Mum, did you notice at your funeral that your son wore his white Royal Australian Naval Reserve uniform to show you what a good man—a real man—he was. Deep down, his homosexuality burdened him throughout his life. I know you and Dad loved him unconditionally and supported him in every way you could. I was surprised and saddened for you, more than him, when you each confided in me separately before you died, that you could never fully understand. Your guilt was palpable, as though it was somehow your fault that he was gay, which some might interpret as implying there was something wrong with him, but I know you didn't mean it that way. It came from your hearts; you never wanted him to suffer as he did. You did not make him gay; he was naturally born that way. Be proud that you scorned his friends' parents, who disowned their gay sons.

I'm sorry, Mum, that I didn't tell you how ill he sometimes was while you were alive. It was one of our sibling secrets. I'm only thankful you and Dad were safe in whatever heaven you found and could not see his mental anguish, which had him hospitalised several times before he died.

Not a Virgin Marriage

My First Husband

Lying flat on his back, sheet between legs,
one bent like a dancer in pirouette
hairy and lithe on white
with black eyes glinting
above pouting, lustful lips.

Don't be shy, he said, sipping whiskey
my crotch in his hand
possession in his heart
I want to see all of you.

Mouth of smoke
and hot liquor breath
he pulled me down till
my stomach heaved,
This man, my husband.

He, so smart in a suit,
I, young and easily fooled
but when the bruising started
I left. Years later

we met in the street.
I always admired you, he said.

One day, towards the end of my life, I had to have a CT
angiogram at Daw Park, which used to be Adelaide's
Repatriation General Hospital, where I often visited my father
in his dying years. Once I was miserably and uncomfortably
in place on the CT bed, the nurse put a plastic ring on my
finger without warning, and my left arm twitched. Clearly
irritated, she spoke straight over my hospital blue-gowned
abdomen to her counterpart on my right, saying, 'She won't
keep still.'

The remark rankled. The woman had not asked me to keep
still. The words she uttered brought the phrase 'veterinary
medicine' to mind. While working as an anthropological
consultant in Darwin's Aboriginal Areas Protection Authority
in the Northern Territory, I learnt that doctors commonly
used that phrase when working with Aboriginal people who
did not speak English. Having interpreters on tap, as a best
practice, was pretty much unheard of back then, so people
were, as the phrase suggests, treated like dumb animals.

On the morning after my angiogram, I woke feeling
profoundly depressed and crying deep, hard tears as my
mind flew back to my first marriage, when my mother-in-
law told her son, my first husband, reassuring him, without
reference to me, as the nurse had done, that she'd be able
to 'do something with this one'. Being spoken over, being
talked about derogatorily like that, is undoubtedly a form of
abuse, mental abuse. She also said, 'She's pretty enough, but
I'll take her in hand.' That mother-in-law wanted to dress

me as though I were a doll and teach me how to behave well enough for her idea of high society. My husband's immediate grinning acquiescence declared loudly that he didn't love me. He might have well said that I was, in fact, a find.

He literally found me in Port Lincoln, where my parents then managed The Pier Hotel. I was the pretty receptionist whom he invited out of the blue one night to go for a drive to the Winter Hill Lookout. 'For the view,' he said. We hadn't been there long when he kissed me, this man thirteen years my senior. I had mixed feelings of fear, insecurity, heart flutters, and excitement, no doubt because Mum had said only a day earlier that it would be nice if I could marry someone like this man. I was stuck for words when his next utterance took the form of a marriage proposal.

During our brief marriage, he took his mother's message seriously without a blush. He treated me as though I were utterly useless, chasing me around the house with a knife when a meal I'd cooked for visiting neighbours wasn't to his liking. He'd scream at me when I locked the bathroom door—I was seventeen; he was thirty-one. One night, he came home from work after being away for a week. When he knocked, I called out, 'Who is it?' I was by then in the city alone, in a little flat just off Anzac Highway next to where a big Target shopping precinct later emerged. I was alone and frightened, not expecting him to come home that night. When I finally opened the door, he stepped over the threshold, screaming, 'Who the...*foul language*...else would you expect at this time of night?' He came at me with fists and brown eyes blazing with the madness of jealous anger. I cringed as he beat me till I was black and blue.

Six months later, I opened the door one morning to see my father's loving face. I fell to my knees in tears. He took me home to Port Lincoln, where I felt safe with my family around me, but I couldn't forget that Mum also used to shout to Dad about me at times, in front of me—saying 'For God's sake, you're her father, do something about her.'

When I was young, I couldn't fathom why everyone found me wanting in some way. Mum told me I was like my father, Dad said I reminded him of her; each put the bad bits of the other onto me. That made me wonder whether my first husband thought his cruelty would 'fix' me, or if he enjoyed inflicting harm. It seemed in those years that I was the one so often at fault that I began to believe there was indeed something wrong with me.

You didn't know this, Mum, but after you died, your son, my brother, stayed with me when he came from Canberra for your funeral. The kids had all left home by then, but they would visit. One day, a row ensued, and my youngest son walked away from me for a very long time. I can't remember much more than the fact that we fought. Maybe I accused my brother of being self-indulgent with his grief, and my son, who adored his uncle, wanted to defend him against me. Still, I was in grief too, while carrying the load as I always did. It seemed as though everybody jumped on me. My daughter was there, too. As I recall, she just went quiet, then left.

When my brother and I were finally alone that day, we talked and fought while trying to make up, and I broke down as I'd never done before. I fell to the floor and cried, rocking back and forth, my head between my knees as though I were a little girl sulking. As I wept, my body was wracked with anguish, not only in grief, but in despair. I cried out repeatedly from my depths, 'It's not my fault,' while my brother sat behind me on the floor, clasping me tight in his arms as I rocked in pain, telling me over and over again through tears that he loved me.

As a daughter, I was distraught that I couldn't save my mother from death, and that brought me face-to-face with my failure to meet the standards for being a good woman, wife and mother, let alone daughter. While moving house was, in many ways, a way of running from myself, when I didn't or couldn't move, I ran inside myself to hide there, in shame. As I look back now, my belief that I was responsible for everything and everybody may seem sanctimonious, but it actually stemmed from an innate need to be needed. That was my addiction.

Bush Moments

After living in Sydney for a few years, my beloved aunt's son died in uniform in Vietnam, the day before he was due to fly home on his first furlough. I was young and soon flew home to be with my family. My father had just bought a lease on the Transcontinental Hotel in Oodnadatta with my mother's modest inheritance under an entailed will. Admittedly, my mother was from a generation when women followed their husbands wherever they went, and many let their men manage finances. I never questioned these things. Nor did I think to ask what it meant to Mum to abdicate authority over her money. All Mum said about my dead cousin was that Dad had always been jealous of his siblings, especially that particular sister, the boy's mother.

My aunt drank as much, if not more than Mum, who was a binge alcoholic. In her grief, my aunt drank constantly, leaving a mountain of tall, empty, brown beer bottles around her armchair. She had friends who supported her in the drink, so I had no reservations about leaving my aunt's sad house and was delighted to be joining my parents in their new venture.

I had my twenty-first birthday in the outback. Despite my saying I did not want a party, my parents secretly organised a cake and a festive afternoon with a few townsfolk. They presented me with a giant key roughly wrought in tin by a local man, with the number 21 painted on it and a wide, white satin bow which gave it a touch of elegance for the occasion.

It was during these years that I learnt from gossip that, as a woman, I was locally deemed to be good enough to fuck, but not good enough to marry. Not long before I died, chauvinism in Australia had barely changed. Adolescent private school boys in Melbourne were caught with a more sophisticated classificatory system for girls and young women: wifies, cuties, mid (average), sexual object, get out (dismissal), and—unbelievably—unrapable. Forty private-school, male students had listed their female classmates in this way on a spreadsheet.

I couldn't help wondering in my elder years, when that school scandal broke, whether I might have been more comfortable being called unrapable. When I was a young girl, I not only yearned but truly believed it was a woman's destiny to marry, and the bush labelling left me desolate.

From Oodnadatta, I headed to Darwin for a few years, and there in my early twenties, I had a ball. I learnt to play squash and had an affair with a young British fellow who had driven to Australia from the United Kingdom in a Morris Mini. He ran a water ski school while working for Carl Atkinson, a notorious Territorian famous for deep-sea diving and salvage work, who had befriended him. I spent many pleasant evenings at Doctor's Gully with Carl, who used to tease us all the time, and my British boyfriend. I learnt to ski there. We used to have drinks together in the late afternoon and ski from what was then Atkinson's home in Doctor's Gully, right on the water's edge. Carl used to invite tourists and others to feed the fish that swarmed in, in the early evenings. The place later became home to the Aquascene Fish Feeding Sanctuary.

In the promising years of the sixties, I was a tanned, sun-bleached blonde boat-driver and ski-instructor's helper. I travelled with my man to McMinn's Lagoon near Humpty Doo in the wet season. On the way, water splashed high on either side of his small car as we towed the boat along a muddy, semi-flooded, wet track lined with two or three-metre-high spear grass. The end of the track opened up to a beautiful water-lily-filled lagoon. My partner had built a pontoon there for friends and customers to rest on while they waited for their turn to ski.

We also skied on Yellow Waters in Kakadu quite often in the sixties, well before First Nations rights became known to the public. I lived in an era (and class) of ignorance, with few or no restrictions. Even if I were alive now, I would be too scared to ask what the Traditional Owners or Territory wilderness protectors thought of us skiing where we did back then.

We did so on the advice of local crocodile hunters as to when it was safe. I no longer remember if it was in the dry season or the wet. Both fresh and saltwater crocodiles inhabited those wetlands and nested at different times. The croc hunters were interesting men, a cross between the good looks of Peter Finch and rugged outdoorsmen. They were the sort of sun-tanned, self-reliant, don't-give-a-shit bad guys that women were supposed to love back in the day.

I dumped my British boyfriend when he went to a friend's wedding without me, which made me feel not good enough once again. I left Darwin and returned to Oodnadatta. A month or so later, he arrived at our pub to beg me to marry him. I refused. For me, the moment had passed.

Interestingly, when I met him, he presented as an impoverished young fellow of about twenty-one who had driven his Morris Minor across continents from England to Australia. He later became a prominent Territorian himself and eventually married a friend of mine, whom he took to Europe for their honeymoon. Oh well. That was nearly sixty years ago. I met him once, many years later. He and his wife were fighting about whether to send their children to boarding school. He reminded me of how much I used to grizzle about my mother's drinking, which took me aback. Memory is terribly unreliable. I've since come to understand that I was always too strong-willed and too forthright to make men feel comfortable. In my youth, compliance and care were not part of my female vocabulary.

I loved the outback, the vast desert silence, the heat, the flies and the red earth and blue skies of the Australian bush of my years at Oodnadatta. Many years later, this love found its way into my poems. Likewise, the tropics, between Darwin, where I spent over fifteen years, one way or another, and Sri Lanka, where, much later, I met my third husband.

One of my favourite moments of the Oodnadatta days was showering in the outdoor public showers on an otherwise empty road on flat gibber plains stretching to the horizon between the Oodnadatta Airport and the pub. Solid concrete, no doors, but those hot, high-pressure bore-water showers cleansed us deep down and kept us warm in the cool desert air. A couple of female friends and I often went together or met there after a party or a night with a lover, and we'd stand for what seemed like hours, sharing, grizzling, and giggling as young women do. Sometimes, especially in winter, I'd go alone, just for the sensual wonder of the brisk, cold desert air and the stimulating warmth of the water flow; I thrilled to it all.

Father of Children

I was twenty-seven when I met and married my second husband, the father of my three children. He rocked into the pub in Oodnadatta one day, aged twenty-one, having left the Australian Navy to work out bush with an exploration company. By then, I was a twenty-seven-year-old divorcee with a growing trail of failed relationships, more truthfully described as a history of promiscuity behind me. He used to drive eighty kilometres from his camp to the pub regularly and sit at the hotel's big kitchen table, ogling me with a foolish grin. Yet I accepted his offer to visit the work camp with friends to party (just beers), and we fell into a routine that turned into a whirlwind three-month affair without ever getting to know each other. Then we got married in Adelaide.

I was desperate for a husband and a family of my own and dared not risk losing the opportunity he offered. I wanted marriage and children. At first, I didn't know that my Dutch husband was looking for an attractive woman, preferably someone different, who his parents didn't know, because the

Dutch girl they'd previously set him up with had married his older brother. I was certainly not what they wanted for their second son. The family had arrived in Australia when he was eleven. I was six years older than him and far too brash for them. And I was a divorcee. My parents supported me, although they had misgivings that it was a mismatch of the highest order.

As a newlywed, I invited my in-laws to dinner at our new three-bedroom house on a large block in Morphett Vale, which we'd mortgaged for $11,000. I cooked an Italian feast of spaghetti Bolognese, followed by schnitzel, a tossed salad, and apple pie with cream. My husband's four younger siblings looked to their mother, who was staring at her plate in terrifying silence before declaring that she could 'not eat that' in a broad Dutch accent, at which, not one person at the table dared lift a fork, not even her husband. In the end, they ate only my apple pie. I squirmed in mortification.

Perhaps my new mother-in-law intuited the history of the spaghetti Bolognese. My previous boyfriend's mother taught me to make an authentic Italian meal. I adored her handsome, sexy son who gambled heavily. I ended that romance when his lovely sisters told me that he routinely stole from his mother to feed his addiction.

Despite the first in-law dinner, my mother-in-law and I soon became great friends. I grew to love her dearly, and she taught me everything about caring for babies, of which I knew nothing. She had borne six children to a philanderer who used to say he loved her sister more than her. Imagine living with that.

As adults, my children took two recipes from me: one

was my spaghetti Bolognese, and the other was a pretty convincing version of a creamy white spinach soup I first tasted in Nepal. Yes, I'm jumping years, but my mind works that way and speaking of years, my second husband called several times every year for many, many years to ask for a copy of that Bolognaise recipe as he rotated through subsequent wives and more babies. He'd also contact me annually to ask for our children's birth dates. The only one he could recall was our daughter's, which was the same date as his older brother's. When he visited South Australia for work after I retired there, he'd still call me out of the blue and invite himself for a cuppa at my place when he had a few hours to kill before catching a flight home. Once, he told one of his many wives to ask me for health advice relating to their new baby. He was a funny fellow.

It would break my heart to delve into the details of what went wrong in my second marriage. All I can say is that a combination of immaturity, inexperience, and unmet expectations in both of us took its toll. We never got to know each other as individuals. Love was there, with wishes and unmatched expectations. Still, sex was fraught and having three children in rapid succession meant that we didn't see, let alone meet each other's desires or needs, so gradually the relationship drowned in disappointment, leaving me with three children to raise alone without financial support. There were no laws around such things back then.

Did I love him? Yes, although I was often angry at his immaturity while we were together. For example, after I came home from being a breakfast cook and housekeeper in my parents' pub in town, the Hotel Franklin, he'd still be sound asleep after lunch. One day, I found our first two children, a boy and a girl, born just twelve months and thirteen days apart, sitting unkempt in sodden, stinking nappies on the kitchen floor, having emptied packets of cereal from the kitchen cupboard to eat. If I complained, he'd say, 'Stop nagging.'

I can hear you now, Mum, saying, 'I don't know why you let that man upset you. He just uses you.' Which he always did. If you were here, I'd tell you that I wasn't upset, but I was. Even after he left, his contact enlivened me, and his absence saddened me, and it took me a long time to stabilise after each encounter. I doubt you'd have been surprised that when tragedy entered my life years later, long after you were gone, he immediately and forever ceased communication with me. You always could read me better than I understood myself, though I realised long ago that you really didn't have eyes in the back of your head.

Even in my old age, I wonder why I still feel such a connection with the man I always called my real husband. I would not have liked living with who he became over the years. Nor do I miss him, but I do wonder whether the lingering connection I feel arises from having his children. My gut thinks so. The strange thing is that now, while I might moan a little about the bad bits, my decade with the kid's father lodged itself in my heart like a brilliant but slightly flawed gemstone. After all, he gave me my beautiful, beloved children. The pain comes from being discarded.

On Birthing and Ageing Parents

I had never seen a baby till I had my first child. As a young single woman, the only time I came close was when Mum and I visited our next-door neighbour in hospital after she gave birth. Our feminine gift honoured the new mother, not the baby. When the new mum asked if we'd like to see her baby, my mother said no. She firmly believed there was too much fuss over newborns when they didn't know what was going on. She preferred to celebrate the mother, especially a first-time one. Neither Mum nor I had heard of feminism back then, but I took Mum's view on board until I had my first baby. Only then did I understand how much we want people to admire our little ones.

I had three children, one after the other, so close that Mum announced to all and sundry in the pub where we lived that I was breeding like a rabbit. It brought a boozy laugh from customers. What she didn't know is that I had had three abortions between my first marriage and the second, all illegal. One nearly killed me. I took myself to the Darwin hospital, fainting with excessive blood loss at the Emergency Department entrance. I spent several days alone over Christmas, having my blood levels restored in a hospital bed. I adamantly stuck to my story that it was a miscarriage, a very uncomfortable lie that medical staff accepted grudgingly to save me from a criminal record and up to a decade in prison. For $50, I'd had a sleazy backyard abortionist flush my uterus with a two-litre bucket of soapy water while I lay on a towel on the cold, tiled floor of my tiny hostel room. He left me with instructions to empty the bucket each time it filled with blood in a building where the shared bathroom was a long corridor away.

I flew to Sydney to have the other two abortions at an illegal clinic in the heart of Sydney's Bondi. One time, I remember stepping out of the door, still dozy from the anaesthetic, about an hour after entering, only to bump into two uniformed police officers. I was terrified that I'd be caught. I should mention that the pill didn't exist until 1961, and many young women wouldn't touch it. By an idiotic fifties-type logic, we believed we'd be seen as bad girls if we took it, the outcome of which was that good girls got pregnant. Not that I'm claiming to have been good.

When I married the second time, I was worried that my abortion history might prevent me from conceiving again, especially after consulting a phrenologist in Sydney who declared that I'd never have children. That prediction led my husband and me to a specialist to see if I could, and lo and behold, I was already pregnant and gave birth eight months after we married. The baby was premature—socially lucky, but medically true.

My firstborn was a boy. As we used to say, 'as it should be'. I went into the birthing suite in complete ignorance of the intensity of pain one must endure. I was in second-stage labour for days, listening to other women come, scream and go. Finally, a doctor attended to me, and instead of anaesthetising me for a caesarean section, he ripped me apart. Back then, only after we'd given birth would older women share birthing stories with young mums.

As someone who had always wanted a sister, I had hoped for a girl, but the moment the nurse placed a tiny boy creature in my arms, my heart melted, no matter that he'd spent three days resisting life, making mine extremely painful and tearing my muscles. I had never known the meaning of pure love before that child was born. Reviving the experience on the page brought a flash of realisation: the blending of pain and love while birthing offers a philosophical lesson. It is fundamentally and irreversibly transformative.

One year and thirteen days later, my daughter was born without causing me any distress, except that the staff took a long time to examine her before wrapping her for me to hold in my arms. She also took a while to cry. As before, love flowed from me.

After a two-year respite, my third child was born in Darwin during the wet season in November. He was back in the hospital on Christmas Eve, 1974. My husband and I had been working in my family's pub in Ardrossan, a South Australian country town, where Dad introduced him to football, for which I could have cursed him. We soon left for Darwin to live our own lives after my husband complained that my father was treating him like a messenger boy. He signed up for the NT Police Force, and off we went.

There were other things, too, once I was a mother. My parents changed towards me, as did my gay brother, whose friends used the offensive descriptor, 'breeders', for women like me with children. By dint of having babies, I had become a joke. To my aged horror, many years later, I found that the term 'breeders' persisted in other quarters among childless women, so much for feminism.

Going back, whenever my mother passed my marital bedroom, she'd avert her gaze. I forgave her, as she was from a different era. Other than that, her only input into my life as a new mother was to insist that my babies be left alone in their cribs and not be bothered or handled all the time. Dad's demeanour towards me changed completely. To him, the season of my being his little girl had passed. He began treating me as a woman like any other, a creature that makes men's lives miserable (like his wife). A distance grew between us when he insisted that I become responsible for my brother in his stead, as he always did with Mum. I still had to play peacemaker for him until I had the courage to refuse.

As my parents aged, my children hit their teenage years. When the kids were at school, my parents were generous, buying them desks, bicycles, and more because I received no child support from their father. It was not legally required at the time. Thanks to my parents, my children, apart from not having a father or the swimming pool most fathers were supposed to provide, didn't miss out on much. Even then, I worked part-time and did what I could for my elderly parents while studying full-time and raising three new humans.

Do you remember, Mum, telling me not to fuss over my babies, to let them sleep and learn to be alone so they gain independence? You weren't slow to pick them up to help them up pub stairs, impatiently when they were toddlers, so you were a bit inconsistent in that regard. Still, your nemesis, the paternal grandmother and my husband's mother of six, used to say a similar thing, about being kind but firm. She gave me a Women's Weekly article showcasing Kahlil Gibran, whose words I've never forgotten. 'Our children are not ours,' he said, 'They are the sons and daughters of life's longing for itself'. You both recognised my weakness—dare I admit it—that I wanted my kids to love me, and I failed. Although they were physically cared for, and I truly loved them, I learnt too late that I was only in this life to provide a circle of safety for my children until they could fly happily on their own.

Cyclone Tracy

My second marriage became quite shaky after we moved to Darwin, where my third child, a baby boy, was born. The confinement was problematic; the baby was born in breech, coming into the world, legs first. There were so many doctors and nurses in the room that I could have been a celebrity. But, no, it was a dangerous delivery. Poor little mite spent his first days in an incubator, while I was on bloods, so I had to walk with a drip stand to the nursery to see him. I think it was about ten days later that we brought him home.

On Christmas Eve in 1974, the baby became severely ill with a high temperature and listlessness. When my husband came home from work, I said we should head to the hospital. I was scared. He insisted on going to footy training for a team that was already out of the running for the season finals and left. The infant started convulsing. I called my neighbours (no mobile phone then). As a police family, we had neighbours who were police couples of child-raising age, like us. Despite having little ones and a baby, one husband went to the oval to tell my husband to get to the hospital as I'd taken the baby there. Another left his wife to look after my other two children with her two toddlers and newborn while he took me and mine to hospital. My baby was diagnosed with meningitis and admitted. My husband finally showed up in time to take me home to a house full of guests, because he had failed to cancel a party we'd arranged as I'd asked. When I told them what had happened, they understood and left.

That night, Tropical Cyclone Tracy—Category 4—huffed and puffed and blew our house down. We had followed the batten-down instructions, albeit with a general feeling of equanimity. Darwin gets a lot of cyclones. I'd called my mother, who arrived from Adelaide that evening, with a view to helping with my sick baby when he was discharged from hospital. That never happened.

For the two little ones at home, we played at being cheerful around our decorated Christmas tree, standing tall over shiny-wrapped gifts, but the wind grew strong, whistling its warning, and we went to bed, though sleep was impossible. The wind sounded like an oncoming train as it pounded the house. We all bundled into one room, crammed together on a single bed. As the storm hit its peak, our roof lifted off and blew away. In the morning, when the danger had passed, my husband took us down the rickety stairs (the house was on stilts) one by one to the concrete laundry beneath, which became our temporary sanctuary. A running crier came by, shouting that Tracy might turn back, but it didn't. Soon afterwards, a loudspeaker from a slow-moving vehicle announced that we should head to Casuarina High School for shelter.

Call Me Marigold

Terror was in our hearts until we had news that, although Tracy flattened the hospital, our new baby had been evacuated in time. We were reunited at the airport three days later. Our first evacuation offer was to Alice Springs, but we insisted on waiting until we could travel to Adelaide as a complete family, which we did.

1974

A new house in Darwin,
angels twinkle and bells tinkle
on a fresh pine branch in the corner
while fridge and freezer wheeze
with the weight of kabana and beer,
ham, pork and turkey—
all that Christmas cheer.
Clouds glower. A howl of wind
blows visitors home,
and older children hide gifts
under beds as louvred windows shatter.
The roof lifts off.

A whining, whirring, whinnying wind
batters the house of your mind. Rain
pelts, squalls, gusts at regular intervals,
like a runaway train, it pummels
fibro sheets from their moorings.
Metallic sounds scratch, crash and scrape,
splintered homes were whipped and whooshed
in obeisance to a power
that pelts fridges like ping pong balls
and propels cars into water towers
and pools on hotel roofs.

I want to pee says your two-year-old.
Pee on the bed, you keen as lightning
coruscates the black curtain of tropical stars,
and slivers of frozen rain pierce your face.
You lie in the tiny warm puddle.

After thunder, silence —
the storm's eye.
Will death come tonight?

At dawn, you hustle outside
to a yellow-grey fugue
bereft of birdsong and rustling leaves.
A solitary crier emerges from rubble,
head to the school, he calls, hurry,
Tracy is turning back.

The stinking disappointment of foul meat, sour milk,
melted ice cream and wilted lettuce
rots next to warm booze in fridges across Darwin.

Merry Christmas.
Women pitch in at the shelter,
cook, clean and manufacture nappies
from toilet paper for little ones with the trots.
In the face of disease, you tremble on blankets
beneath giant, jagged guillotines of window glass
loose enough to drop any moment.

Three days and three nights
communications were down,
a doctor hides his skills under blankets
till exposed for stealing a plate of eggs
scrambled with powdered milk for kids.
There is a kerfuffle, but women

Call Me Marigold

and children keep going with measles
while men do what they can,
out and about.

Just as planes come to whisk you away
you hear that someone down the road
was sliced in two by a meteor
of corrugated iron. You wonder
if it was from your roof,
light a cigarette and pray.

A man in female garb is arrested
as 360 women, children and babies
board a Boeing 727; its capacity, 180.
Tighten your seatbelts, the hosties plead
as the plane's tail dips its nose points to heaven
from the weight of the line to the loo.
Laughter erupts.
Even the hosties were scared.

Pier Street

Soon after resettling in Adelaide, we leased a deli in Pier Street, Glenelg, with the $3000 Commonwealth Government resettlement grant we received for surviving Cyclone Tracy. Two years later, I found that I was still easily scared when Don Dunstan stood on the Glenelg Pier after news of a possible tsunami hitting Adelaide. It takes a while for fear to dissipate after a disaster. When our seven-day-a-week deli became too much for us, we sold it and bought a house in Hastings Street, Glenelg. Soon after that, in 1979, my husband deserted me.

At first, I couldn't sleep for days because I was frightened. What if a man (they're always men in one's fear-filled imaginings) broke into the house, or some creepy thing happened? I was desolate, a terrible sense of isolation at not having anybody to lean on (a fantasy in fact). Interestingly, people told me I was better off without my husband. Someone suggested I see a doctor. My GP prescribed Xanax, a Benzodiazepine. After one little blue pill, I flaked out on my bed in the daytime, only to wake up to three distraught little children crying for mummy and shaking me to wake up. I swore off such poisons for life.

That experience changed me. I grew angry that medical advice was to dispense pills to mask natural feelings like grief or, in my case, to pacify a woman who could have done with support. It was a wake-up call for me to get a grip and be present for my family. I came to believe that, if we allow pain to be as it is without judgment, it is the essence of recovery.

I had no income, and I had to make my first-ever visit to Social Security (now Centrelink). They gave me a Widow's Pension. The Social Worker was kind. I even got a small grant to buy Christmas gifts for my children. Not long afterwards, my brother, by then a ballet dancer, offered me work in the ballet school he had set up in a de-sanctified church in Whitmore Square. Our parents had helped him establish it in partnership with a prominent Adelaide dancer. Slowly, I got back on my feet.

I'd hoped my children would stay with me until their twenties, perhaps go to university, but they all left home relatively young. My daughter was sixteen, and my eldest son was seventeen. The youngest stayed until he was nineteen. I had yearned for freedom, but it didn't work like that. I had to learn to let go and allow my children to find their own paths. I had to adjust to the loss of that integrated feeling of belonging in this world, of having a role, and of being wanted and needed. I had empty-nest syndrome.

If I could speak to my children now, I'd say, I wish I'd been a better mum. My parents, brother, and in-laws all told me I was a good mother, and that my offspring wanted for little. I fed, clothed and housed them well. I loved them beyond life itself. But I can see now that I didn't let my love show. I scolded them and was probably strict, as my mother had been with me. I told myself I was a consultative mother and asked them to sit at our round kitchen table for weekly family conferences. Many years later, they laughed and told me I had only brought them together to let them know what I wanted from them. They could see something in me that I didn't know about myself.

We had fun at times. Especially memorable for me were those sweltering hot nights when we hauled mattresses onto the back lawn with the dog and cat, to sleep under the stars. I loved our weekend trips to places like Cleland National Park in the Adelaide Hills and Victor Harbour on the Fleurieu Peninsula. Often on a Sunday morning, they'd come to my bed, and we'd play, but I kept my true feelings of insecurity, sadness and melancholy inside instead of being real. I was probably more concerned with ticking the right mothering boxes—which was about me—than showing them how to be true to themselves.

The outcome of having an extremely difficult last confinement was a hysterectomy. I wasn't going to include this story, but I wanted to show how medical sexism worked in my day. Aside from my post-cyclone fear, I was unwell. I agonised for days about what to do and how to tell a doctor about my problem. You see, my uterus had prolapsed and externalised. Eventually, I found the courage to see a local doctor. I took a little piece of paper on which I'd written a list of concerns because my hair was falling out and, among other things, I had an infection.

Without examining me, the doctor immediately and with great distaste gave me an urgent referral to a psychiatrist.

The psychiatrist was horrified and referred me just as urgently to a gynaecologist, and, within a week, I had a hysterectomy.

I then had to see the same GP for a post-operation checkup, and I happened to mention that my husband was impatient for sex, which I could not tolerate after vaginal surgery. The GP prescribed an anaesthetic gel.

University

I left school in 1958, at the age of fifteen and, in 1980, aged thirty-seven, entered the University of Adelaide as a special-entry tertiary student. The entrance exam for those who didn't qualify based on school results was essay-based. I had to write five hundred words—the most I'd ever put together in my life. Most of the questions made no sense, so I answered the only one that did. It asked why I should be admitted. Full of the wisdom of ignorance and with my quintessential quick wit and smart answers honed as a publican's daughter, I concluded my essay with a question that went something like this: How could my education be wasted when I have three small children?

So, there I was on campus, a single mother of three, working part-time and studying full-time at the University of Adelaide, later tutoring and lecturing for several years, culminating in a PhD. For more than a decade, I led a distinctly divided life. Until I won a Commonwealth scholarship for my PhD, half of me earned money cooking breakfasts and doing the housework at my parents' pub (and others around Glenelg at times) while raising children at home. The other half was on campus, where I often yearned to be at home with my babies. When I was alone at home for too long, I yearned to be back among my knowledgeable and fun new friends, learning about life and the world. I became addicted to learning. I read everything on the curriculum, and more, as mature students often do. My PhD proposal had ten pages of citations, which impressed at the time.

I thought university would offer relief from being mocked or told I was either stupid or wrong. But, where my first and second husband's put-downs were like a dripping tap that tortured my confidence and self-belief, many people at university mocked me because I held wrong views. For example, I was politically naïve and failed to understand why people fussed about women getting a lesser wage than men, which, even looking back, was never evil, but in its time, was predicated on the principle that men were breadwinners supporting wives and children at home. It wasn't until my second year at university that feminism transformed my life and understanding. Feminism taught that the personal is political, and as Emile Durkheim said of suicide, private suffering is a social fact, not an individual flaw, as I'd always thought.

Although I became an active feminist for a time, my life remained compartmentalised. Scholarly learning in the public sphere and living in the world as I knew it did not easily fit together for me. Guilt created a rift between the exciting exploration of new worlds and ideas, and the isolation, loneliness and heavy responsibility of being a single mum to three kids. In practice, as opposed to theory, the worlds of politics, knowledge, mothering, and, later, caring for one's ageing parents did not easily meld. Reflecting on this reminded me of something interesting I learnt while interviewing my parents in their old age.

Towards the end of my postgraduate years, I wanted to document aspects of their lives, the people, events and places that they had loved and valued. Their totally different responses surprised me, not so much for the content, as I was familiar with the details. What fascinated me was how differently they anchored themselves in the world when they told their stories and how they understood themselves within it. Dad recounted his life, touching on Japan and the post-World War II years, of course, plus political events, footy grand finals, and the races. Mum inextricably linked her story to her childhood, her two sisters, who married whom and when, and when her mother died. The contrast was stark. When I asked them to recall the place where they were happiest. Dad chose Japan, where he had achieved significant social status as an army major after growing up in poverty, walking three miles to and from school every day. Mum selected Oodnadatta, where, in her middle years, she made friends with other women for the first time.

Going to university meant my life was bifurcated between my public persona as a tertiary student and my role as a mother. Neither world fitted easily into the other. A young male colleague, a graduate student, once told me I should embrace single motherhood instead of living my life as though I were half of a nuclear marriage. Ouch. That remark, unkind in its delivery, made me realise that I had to change, but how? Another male graduate student stopped speaking to me altogether after the department head assigned me three of the five available postgraduate tutorials. The extra class had to go to someone, but the guy was livid, arguing that it was a form of discrimination based on my having three children. Back then, feminism still had a way to go. Equality is not absolute.

I had no plans or goals when I entered university. I loved my early years there, a new life, friends and discovery. I couldn't resist pursuing Honours in anthropology and got a First. By then, I was tempted to sign up for a postgraduate course in Social Administration at Flinders University as a path to a well-paid future. It would have been the responsible thing to do. How different my life would have been had I taken that path, but my romance with anthropology was deep and abiding. Like any powerful love, it drew me away from common sense and deeper into an understanding not only of our world but also of others', with a touch of philosophy and creativity thrown in. I was hooked. Little did I know what was to come.

Having written about Sri Lanka for my Honours thesis, I had also fallen in love with that country through earlier travel and research. I was thrilled at the prospect of living overseas with my three children for an eighteen-month stint of postgraduate fieldwork.

It was a trip that changed my life.

My Third Husband

After travelling to Sri Lanka post-Honours with a couple of other student friends, purportedly to meet our professor, who was a specialist in Sri Lanka and then on the island, I wanted to work, as he had, with ritual practitioners, drummers, dancers, and acrobats, and learn about their performative celebrations of gods and demons. I had a fascination with South Asian ritual and religion, and I wanted to understand what it all meant to the people who practised such rites in a Buddhist nation. The task was as tantalising as it was challenging.

My three children, then nine, eleven, and twelve, were with me, so the first thing to do was find someone to cook, clean, and look after them while I was away from home for a few days at a time, attending all-night rituals in jungle villages. In Sri Lanka, this meant having a servant. My landlord found me a perfect woman to whom I willingly entrusted my children. I adored her.

In my PhD thesis, I acknowledged my three children thus—

Their beautiful, inquisitive, and effervescent youth attracted many people to us as a family, which made them excellent sources of new friends and colloquial information. Both boys were fascinated by the unique rhythms of Sri Lanka's ritual music and dance, and before long, they were eager to learn these for themselves. The eldest was deeply disappointed that he could not because, like my daughter, he was committed to his schooling and, even at 12, was taller than many of the ritual practitioners. My youngest son was of a much smaller build, so he became a pupil of a ritual practitioner with international fame, who became my husband. (Names elided.)

My third husband, whom I loved dearly, died many years ago, but I was fortunate, once Facebook came into being, to receive friend requests from his children in Sri Lanka, who, of course, now have grown children of their own. We remained in touch, and my kids no doubt would have let them know of my recent demise.

Like many Westerners, I fell in love with Sri Lanka and its people. Only belatedly did I understand that there was something wrong about saying that. Such statements infantilise and objectify entire nations and groups of people. They are, effectively, racist. They feel pure-hearted, but it is the same as a man saying, 'I'm not sexist because I love women.' Or women similarly saying, 'I love men'—plural. The question always is, which one? It suddenly became clear to me that stereotypes obscure personality and character, the very things that make us human.

I also realised that there was a contradiction at the heart of anthropology. Falling in love with 'the other' was frowned upon in a discipline that, by studying humans, was by definition objectifying them, often categorising, which is to say, stereotyping. It's one thing to observe others and form judgments, and quite another to be among people as an outsider in order to study them and write theses or gain fame with what we think we learn. Marrying in the field had me questioning the nature of relationships like mine.

It also raised concerns for me about fieldwork as such. We all fall for the cultures we work in, but back then, we rarely studied people in other cultures for their sake. Instead, we sought to enrich the body of so-called Western knowledge and gain acclaim through our research findings. In the end, for me to marry someone in the field was, to put it bluntly, a bad career move. Male anthropologists may litter the world with their offspring, but as a woman, I broke the rules.

How did we get together?

My fieldwork took me deep into jungle villages to attend rituals for the Goddess Pattini called Gam Maduwa, or loosely translated, Village Palace. It was a time in my life when I felt vulnerable as a woman and still hoped to find love.

Living in this fragile context left me vulnerable and, instead of rising to the academic status conferred on me by the Sri Lankan people, I succumbed to my inner yearnings. Although I was a mere fledgling academic, they referred to me as Dr, but my social boundaries fell away with a man who, for his own reasons, wanted to come to Australia with me. He once said to me that love has no barriers. He was right. However, the world always wants people to be where they are supposed to be. Forming a liaison with an informant, as we patronisingly described the people we studied in the

Discipline of Anthropology, was supposed to be kept secret, not formalised in marriage.

In Sri Lanka, I pondered deeply on the ethics of my profession. Ethical guidelines for conducting research with humans were not introduced into the social sciences until the National Statement on Ethical Conduct by the National Health and Medical Research Council was released in 1999. That was after I left academic life and was working in Aboriginal health services in Katherine, in the Northern Territory. But even in the 1980s, my research in Sri Lanka raised issues for me. My concern was not only that I married while in the field, but also with the whole structure of participant observation as a practical model for research.

I can't believe it wasn't until I said goodbye to my eldest son when he left home for England at eighteen to follow a girlfriend that I completely understood the desolation hiding behind your and Dad's bright smiles and brittle goodbyes when I, and my three children, left for Sri Lanka. We were all a bit giggly and teary, weren't we? When I returned to Australia, you told me I'd changed. You insisted that I used to be a happy, smiling little girl, and I'd lost that. What a portent that was. Like you, albeit for different reasons, I became serious, if not humourless, in old age, and often suffered what doctors called anhedonia. But that was much later.

The Perahera

Sri Lanka's Asala Peraharas were glorious processions held on the full moon of Asala in the Buddhist calendar of full moon (*Poya*) days, all of which celebrate a special event in the life of the Buddha. The Asala Perahara coincided with the end of the Buddhist monks' annual three-month retreat. For tourists, they were a cultural showcase of traditional arts and crafts with drummers, dancers, acrobats, and flamethrowers parading alongside gloriously caparisoned elephants carrying the Buddha's Tooth (the Dalada), housed in Kandy's Temple of the Tooth. In history, this rite bound Buddhism and royalty in a symbiotic relationship, with monks praising good kings and kings patronising the Buddhist Order.

Where once the Kandy Perahara was an exclusive royal event, over time Asala Peraharas proliferated across Sri Lanka. I called it the democratisation of a ritual once reserved for royalty after my Sri Lankan husband chuckled one day and said, 'Nowadays, everyman is king.' The principle remains that offering or funding any ritual, let alone a large ritual procession like an Asala Perahara linked politicians and businessmen to various sects within the Buddhist Order and created enormous prestige.

The Tourist

It's not my country...
        this jewelled isle of caparisoned elephants
       and twirling dancers, chanting and
      torch throwing in dazzling costumes
     over pure white cloth
      to a million torches and drums
       thrumming in veneration
        Buddhist spectacle surround sound.

It's not my country...
       where obeisance to gods
      and vows are performed
     in coconut frond palaces
      woven for the divine when
       a priest trans vests to dance
        in silken sari and trance. He is the Goddess.
         Cries of joy and rupees adorn Her sacred hem.

It's not my country...
       where drunken tourists
      lounge near-naked in hotel luxury
     and palm-lined beaches
      wander unheeding in
       paddy fields people call home
        where buffalo graze and children play.
        Passport to selfies on Instagram.

Call Me Marigold

It's not my country...
    where strangers ask, *Madam, you are from?*
    Do you want hashish, madam?
    Boys, sir?
    On streets where monks and guns parade.

It's not my country...
    where village souls at first meeting
    take you to their mud-brick home
    where children laugh and women
    squat at hearth making chai.
    Though poor, they share their meal with a smile.

No, it's not my country...
    where begging and touting
    remind us daily that
    to give is a blessing.
    No. It's a piece of my heart.

My Three Divorces

Emotional turbulence played havoc with me when I returned from Sri Lanka. Not that I had any inkling at first, but things were about to change, not only because middle age and menopause were quickly creeping up on me, but because I lost the loving comfort of my third husband's arms when he returned to his home country, leaving me alone once again with my three children, who were becoming increasingly mysterious beings called teenagers, and with ageing parents. My personal life was a blur of distress and anxiety, trying to hold it together as I completed my PhD while teaching full-time.

As each year passed, however, my most fraught moments began to transform until they no longer carried judgment and pain. I was never certain how or why that happened, but the sad and bad parts of my life became treasured experiences. I suspect that the solitude of my years in the bush may have contributed to my thinking this way, not to mention many years of meditation. One of those pieces was my 'collection' of divorces.

My first divorce took three years and a bit before the Decree Absolute was issued in absentia. The three waiting years were happy for me, living in Darwin, where I learnt to water ski and play squash. I worked for the government as a typist and stenographer. I even worked as a court reporter at times. Once, I was called in to record a Royal Commission into a case concerning a government employee who spoke out about something the government felt was detrimental to it. I used a lead pencil for shorthand, then transcribed my notes using an upright Imperial typewriter for the record.

In those early Darwin days, I lived in a hostel for government employees, with casual friendships and pub and room parties on tap. It was in that hostel that I had the three illegal abortions mentioned earlier. I guess I went a little overboard with the new freedoms of the 1960s.

My second divorce, just under a decade later, was orchestrated in no small part by my would-be hippy and ballet-dancing brother, who insisted that my soon-to-be second ex and I meet him in a bar after court to celebrate like friends. That meeting nearly killed me. I needed to cry, shout in anger at the unfairness of this world, and otherwise slump into self-pity for a while. My loving but naïve gay brother believed that wrong in a marriage was always on both sides. I didn't like his logic. I wanted to be, and often felt like a victim. I had been deserted, left alone to fend for three kids, minus income support. 'You are both nice people,' he'd say, 'but you just weren't a good fit.'

It took me most of my life to let that idea enter me, especially after the custody hearing, where my suitability as a mother was savagely questioned by the court before I was allowed—note the term—to keep my children. At the time, I couldn't believe my ears. Their father didn't attend. It was beyond my comprehension that a pompous old man in a wig (he didn't wear one, I added that for effect) would question my sobriety, my love for my children, and my capacity to house and care for them as though I were a criminal.

My ex soon disappeared from South Australia to live interstate. Like me, he remarried several times. Unlike me, he added several more children to the world. I changed my name back to my maiden name and added it to my children's legal names in a way that allowed them, had they wanted, to use a double-barrelled surname. My logic was that he broke our contract, and I raised them alone, even though, in many ways, that was a blessing.

I prepared and issued divorce papers to my third husband at the Adelaide Legal Aid Services Commission, which offered free do-it-yourself divorce forms. My third husband and I had an amicable separation, much as my brother had envisaged long ago for my second marriage. It was a simple formality hardly worth mentioning, except to say I have a propensity to be orderly and like to formalise things.

Talking about divorces reminded me of what you said about my last affair, Mum. He was a philanderer in his marriage, a professional colleague of mine and a thorough bastard. Yet, I believed I was in love with him and hoped that my middle years might deliver my slowly dying dream of having a loving partner in life. But dreams can be cruel. He had another partner on the side, while professing his lifelong love for his erstwhile wife to both of us.

Do you remember what you said when I told you, Mum? Your words were, 'Just chew 'em up and spit 'em out.' In other words, if the sex is good, take it and forget the rest. I have to laugh at your carnal forthrightness in old age, after a lifetime pretending sex didn't exist. I guess the forced abstinence of your marriage was painful to bear.

On Rape

Between my late teens and early twenties, I was raped three times, twice in Port Lincoln and once in Oodnadatta. Like most aspects of my life, good, bad and sad, these problematic moments fossilised over time. Let's say these particular stings fossilised in amber.

The Oodnadatta experience was, you might say, violent in the true sense. I wasn't beaten, but I was hurt. It happened during Race Week, held annually in May, when I was walking home from the Race Week Ball, now known nationally as a Bachelor and Spinster ball. I was, of course, the publican's daughter, and having worked hard all week, I was tired, so I left the ball early. The music, dancing, laughter and heightened sexual atmosphere were too much for me that night. For the bush people, it was an annual event that brought the district together to search for love or matchmake, but gossip had already told me that I was not marriage material in that crowd. I walked home slowly along the red-dirt main street of that tiny outback town, dreaming under the moonlight and flotilla of stars floating above me, ready for bed but content.

As I turned the corner towards the pub's back gate, a man with red hair, whom I recognised from the bar as a railway fettler, was standing as though he was waiting for me. He caught me in his arms, threw me onto my back on a bed of stones and took me without consent. He pumped so hard for a long time, then left me lying there, bleeding. For a while, I lay stock still in bewilderment before gathering the strength to go home and hide my ripped clothing. I then stood under a steaming hot shower for over an hour. I never told a soul that my back was black and blue with ugly bruises that didn't fade for weeks.

A week or so later, my mother remarked that I'd wash my skin off if I kept showering so often. Without being aware, I'd fallen into the habit of taking a shower morning and night, and sometimes in between. I just shrugged her words off and became surly. I don't think she ever guessed what had happened.

Earlier, when I was about sixteen in Port Lincoln, an awkward grappling by an old man in his sixties, who pushed his hardness on me from behind, while standing up with trousers on, as his hands crept beneath my nickers to work my crotch, in an enclosed space that I can't fully recall. Maybe the cloak room of the Pier Hotel? It was Race Week, and I may have been returning his coat. He ejaculated into his trousers and then stumbled away. I later discovered he was a well-known TV personality.

The other, equally revolting incident at that time was when a musician at least fifteen years my senior, a pianist who sometimes played for the pub's dinner dances, crept into my bedroom upstairs and pushed himself into me as I slept. When I woke, I struggled unsuccessfully to push him away, and he came with unseemly jerks and groans. Immediately afterwards, he climbed off me, tucked his penis into his undies, pulled his pants up from his ankles (he'd left his shoes on!) and slithered out of the room without a word. For those who did not grow up in pubs, be assured that this bedroom-slither thing was not uncommon. I locked my bedroom door forever after. I feared pregnancy, but I was lucky.

Back then, the gender ground was ripe for rape. The joking language towards naïve and nubile young women back then would put men in gaol nowadays. I include these episodes, which I never shared with anyone until I was in my forties and found a couple of close women friends to talk to, because rape steals your autonomy, and it shames you.

Working in a bar with drunks, I was fresh game. I learnt to fend off most crudity with my refined habit of quick wit and smart answers. I refused to suffer fools lightly, yet all that smart-Alec language was a mask. Inside, I was retiring and even secretive about many things. In the government hostel where I lived in Darwin for several years in my twenties, other young women found me weird because I didn't share personal 'girly' stuff. What they didn't know was that I'd been raised to think that keeping company and going out with other women was seen as a sign that you couldn't get a man. Goodness knows where that idea came from. They were innocents, and though no fault of my own, I wasn't.

Lindy Warrell

The Shame

I get mad very mad you guessed it I am cross and angry and pissed-off not to speak of beside myself whenever I hear about you know rape that thing men force onto women who don't want it who say no but men don't get it they do not understand the English language and the meaning of words like no go away bugger off or stop which is a red word but do you think it makes a difference of course not it seems to attract like a rag to a bull in a China shop whatever that means but they do say not to wear red around a bull so perhaps if we say go for it mate in green it might scare them half to hell after all if they are not taking maybe they'll find they didn't want it in the first place that v-jay-jay that lovely sacred soft spot in a woman that can be so inviting to those who are welcome you often wonder don't you if he'll be perfumed or gross but when you want him it doesn't matter and when you don't it's all the fucking same full of shame not his but yours why's that do you reckon?

Mum's Death and North Queensland

When I first worked as a private anthropological consultant with First Nations people (then known as Aboriginal people), I frequently drove miles across South Australia, the Northern Territory and Queensland, where I met generous souls who, after they became comfortable with me, had me record their stories for land clearances and, in some cases, posterity. Even years later, after working far off-road with various groups, I prided myself on being able to recognise parts of the Australian landscape on social media with near 100% accuracy. Our deserts, scrublands, mountain ranges, and gibber plains offer subtle variations in shapes and labile shades of red, ochre, and purple, along with a profusion of colours in leaves and bark.

I didn't get around to buying a four-wheel drive, a vehicle that became a body prototype for an SUV, a city mother's survival kit. Those shiny new vehicles supposedly protected children from accidents while carrying golf clubs, baby carriers, groceries, and dogs. What they lacked were the low-range gearing and locking differentials needed for seriously rugged terrain. A tad dismissively, I thought of SUVs as expensive ornaments. Maybe I was jealous because I raised my children for twenty years in a little red Toyota Corolla station wagon until you could see the bitumen through holes in the floorboards. What stories that car could tell.

Back on topic, for consultancies, I hired a Nissan Patrol or a Toyota Land Cruiser. There was a lot to pack: clothes, maps, paperwork, books, a camera, eskies, tarpaulins, a portable barbecue, a first-aid kit, a billy, my swag, and a laptop. I had my own GPS, a clunky thing in those days that had to be reset each time I crossed a state border or entered a new region. Maps were often more reliable. I used an Ericsson mobile phone, and when they introduced an internet-enabled option, I was among the first in my circle to get one. I was always partial to a bit of high-tech and stayed that way till the end.

In those fieldwork days, CDs were still relatively new in Australia, and radio (I grew up saying wireless) was often out of range, so I developed the habit of driving in silence. I loved driving with the windows down, listening to the variations in wheel sounds on bitumen, sand, dirt, and stony terrain, or in the slippery squelch of mud. Along the way, when trees were around, I'd get wafts of eucalyptus, and I loved the touch of hot, dry or even humid air on the skin of my arm out the window. In my later years, my driving was confined to air-conditioned cars, where I listened instead to the silent workings of my mind, observing, thinking, and making up stories. When I occasionally opened the windows for wafts of eucalyptus, memories flooded back, albeit in bits and pieces, never in chronological sequence.

I can't mention those old GPS systems without immediately thanking Apple and CarPlay, with Siri guiding the way. (I became and remained a Mac girl.) I was glad to see oceans of trees' worth of outdated street directories hit the tip, until I learnt that, as it came of age in my final years, AI consumed masses of the earth's freshwater. Each step forward creates a new problem to solve.

One of the most interesting areas I worked in with First Nations people was in central Queensland, where a new gas pipeline was proposed to run from near Windorah in the West to Brisbane in the East via Eromanga, Quilpie, Charleville, Mitchell, and ending in Roma. My home base was Windorah, just a two-and-a-half-hour drive west of Eromanga, the furthest point from the ocean in all directions in Australia. You can't get more outback than that.

My client had pre-arranged meetings for me with local First Nations groups in each town, to take me out to often-secret, sacred parts of their country. To secure development clearance, they had to identify and justify their relationship with the areas that needed protection. As you would expect in these situations, trust was an issue. Building it quickly in such an environment was never easy. Personality and gender played a role, but more often, once people had time to engage with you and see how you behaved, they'd open up to the extent they were comfortable. I had previously learnt to call the inspection period 'going fishing'. An Elder once gave me that concept when they saw I was struggling to get off the ground.

In those roving years, I learnt so much, not only about respect for country, but also about myself. While taxing at times, working across this land with First Nations people was an immense privilege. If the pressure to behave in acceptable ways and a shrinking contractual timeline ever threatened to overwhelm me, I had to remind myself what it must be like for them to reveal private traditional knowledge to a stranger whose role it was to record it for the public record. How intrusive. But they had little option. To refuse to cooperate would leave their sacred sites exposed to destruction. There have been instances where mining companies have not brought due diligence to the protection process. Some companies thought nothing of deliberately destroying World Heritage sites. The only penalty was financial.

A few days before the pipeline project was due to begin, two local Aboriginal Elders offered to take me to see the surrounding landscape. We spent three days beyond the reach of communication. The places we visited were not on the pipeline route or near any sacred site relevant to the project. Maybe the Elders were sussing me out, but they were three of the best days I've ever had. They took me to Durham Downs, a vast cattle station on Cooper Creek in the Channel Country. That landscape was awe-inspiring in situ, and even more so when I checked aerial maps that revealed the tantalising intricacies of the many waterways in that part of Queensland (and down to South Australia's desert Lake Eyre, which occasionally filled from that river system).

The two Elders gave me the gift of travelling to Cooper Creek itself, which was then dry and sandy. We walked the empty riverbed in silence, listening to the rustle of gum leaves and birds, a desert song. I cherished that moment. It gave me the shivers. Later, they took me miles in another direction. I had no real idea of where I was when we arrived at a vast traditional rock formation that, until 1994, when the first Encyclopaedia of Aboriginal Australia was published, had been unknown outside the local Indigenous populations.

Our next stop in the heat of the day was to swim in a cool, muddy dam. At night, all I had to do was roll out my swag. The Elders built a fire, boiled the billy, and put steak and onions on a blackened barbecue plate they had secreted in the bush for convenience. This was a place where they had camped many times before. They had given me three days of their time, just showing me around. They must have wanted to get to know what sort of person I was, but what they gave me was a life memory. It was not the first time I'd slept out bush in a swag, but lying beneath a vast blue-black sky glittering with more stars than anyone could imagine always made me feel safe, cocooned, and joyful.

We got back to Windorah late in the evening. Early next morning, I took a phone call from my brother. Mum had died overnight. When one of the Elders arrived to meet me on the first day of the project, I told him I had to go home for a few days because my mother had passed away. The Elder replied with deep compassion, 'That old girl couldn't wait, hey?'

I had to hurry. We'd used my hire vehicle for our trip, and although we'd filled it up once, the tank was nearly empty after our long drive. And, it was Sunday, so I couldn't refuel in Windorah. My new friends convinced me I had just enough in the tank to get to Eromanga. It was close, but they were right. I then had to drive to Quilpie, a couple of hundred kilometres further east, to catch a Rex Airlines flight to Brisbane. The next morning, after overnighting with two of my children who were then living in Brisbane, I caught an early flight home to arrange my mother's funeral with my brother, who flew in from Canberra on the same day.

On my return trip, I timed it so I could connect in Brisbane with a flight back to Quilpie to pick up my vehicle and return to Windorah. There were no sick days on a consultancy project, and this one had a tight deadline. I froze. I couldn't cry. My mind was blank, and sleep eluded me. Desperate, I called a friend, who gave me marvellous advice: go out of town, sit beneath a gum tree, allow myself to feel, and stay there until tears came. It worked and, although grief crept up on me several times during that complex project, meeting four different communities with various views over a period of several weeks, I was at least able to function.

I was bereft when you died, Mum. I wish you had waited for me to get back so I could see you one last time. Guilt filled me as though I should have saved you, as I always did. Dad raised me to believe you were my responsibility in your old age, as he did when you drank heavily. I used to wish I could improve your mood, to make him comfortable. During your final years, I hoped I'd done enough by frequently calling and visiting at least once a week. Your son, my darling brother, was too far away and his mental health issues were too paralysing for him by then to help either of us.

Even before you died, I, too, spun around in the cauldron of life, unravelling for a while. Yes, the money you left allowed both my brother and me to put a deposit on a home. Dad let us have it early because he said he didn't need it at the War Veterans' Home. But I lost my house, and what I had become was no more. What I was about to be had yet to show itself. Relief came when I understood that your suffering had ended. It meant I had to be responsible for myself, by myself. I no longer had the option of blaming you. As my youngest son said, 'You're next off the rank, Mum'.

Three years after I lost my mother, Dad died. He had been living in the Fullarton War Veterans' Home for some time after initially taking a respite there. It was Dad's choice to go there to get away from Mum, and she encouraged him for the same reason. The move functioned like a divorce of convenience. Mum visited him with me a few times, but soon stopped. I think they were both relieved of the burden of each other after fifty-odd, often miserable years. The only thing that held them together was loyalty. Maybe that was a form of love.

Mum had a good crowd at her funeral, mostly from the Kapara Nursing Home, where she had been for a year or so. Her middle sister's son, my cousin and his wife attended from Melbourne, and there were lots of flowers. Dad's passing was barely acknowledged, with only five people in attendance. I was there, of course, as was my youngest son and brother. My other two children were both abroad. The daughter of Mum's friend in the booze, who had been my friend, brought her daughter, but the way they behaved and whispered to each other told me they came more out of curiosity than concern. It was a terribly lonely affair.

On Work and Hindmarsh Island

The Advertiser
Caught by Circumstance

By Penelope Debelle 3 February 1996
(NB the subject's name in this press article has been changed from the original copy.)

Drawn by coincidence into the Hindmarsh Island Bridge controversy, anthropologist DR MARIGOLD says she is paying a high price.

The fallout from the Hindmarsh Island saga is still being felt. So far, it has done inestimable harm to public confidence in Aboriginal claims, undermined the independence of anthropologists who appeared to take sides and damaged the careers of individuals.

Adelaide anthropologist Dr Marigold, who was named in the Royal Commission as the possible inadvertent source of the secret women's business, is unemployed. She has barely worked in two years, her dream house at Carrickalinga, with its tranquil study and Eastern artefacts, is for sale, and she fears her career is badly damaged.

The experience has shaken to its roots Dr Marigold's faith

in the career she began as a single mother, bringing up three children.

'I believe we are exploited badly, not listened to and poorly understood,' she says of anthropologists today. 'And if you are labelled in any way, you can be dropped...'

Although her association with Hindmarsh Island was tangential, she says, circumstances elevated it to a seminal status it should never have had. The story began in early 1994 when, out of professional curiosity, she visited the Aboriginal-run tourism project at Camp Coorong. While chatting with the couple who ran it, she said what a pity women's business, women's traditionally separate ceremonial observance, had been left out of the Hindmarsh Island claim. She gave them her card and left. About two weeks later, to her private amusement, the first mention was made of the secret women's business.

During the Royal Commission, the developer, Wendy Chapman, decided, against the wishes of Dr Marigold to present this as something which may have caused the women's business to emerge. 'She rang me and asked if she could use that story,' Dr Marigold says. 'I

said no, it's absolutely pointless, it has no relevance. I told her repeatedly she was barking up the wrong tree. Lo and behold, she used it in the Commission.'

In the Royal Commission findings, the following judgment was made—

'The juxtaposition of this (Marigold's visit to the Coorong) incident with the fact of the emergence of secret women's business two weeks or so later may be just another coincidence. On the other hand, it may have been the occasion on which the seed of 'women's business' was planted.' In other words, Dr Marigold may have started the whole thing.

Marigold is astounded by it all. She had turned the Coorong incident into a party joke, laughing that she had the power to influence the course of events. Not for one moment did she take the connection seriously. 'It's my personality, it's the way I am to take it like that,' she says. 'For it to be taken seriously is absolute bull. . . from beginning to end.' As an anthropologist, she strongly opposed the Royal Commission process and wrote to tell them so. Her belief that it was an impossible forum for assessing the Hindmarsh Island claims Is at the heart of her understanding of anthropology as an evolving study of cultural belief. Just because one history is true, she says, does not mean the opposing view is not. Similarly, neither side on Hindmarsh Island was wrong or right, she says, yet out of the Royal Commission process one side had to triumph.

'They moved straight into a legal situation that is, by definition, adversarial,' she says. 'And it pivots on the notion of truth and untruth as absolutes and there are no absolutes, certainly not in this one.'

In a commissioned review of the report done by fellow anthropologist Dr Deane Fergie (which contained the secret women's business), Dr Marigold criticised as inflammatory the use of sealed envelopes. This was a wrong strategy, she says.

'There shouldn't be any material written down anthropologically that cannot be heard. That's a nonsense. Why seal it up?'

A better option, she says, would be to stop and move into a different forum which could accommodate it. 'In the Northern Territory they do this all the time,' she says.

What she personally believes

about the Hindmarsh Island women's business does not matter, she says. Her background is not theirs and her frames of reference are different. Marigold grew up in Japan, where her parents ran a hotel for the British occupying forces and did her PhD at Adelaide University, on religion in Sri Lanka.

'They are not my stories,' she says. 'What I believe is that the people who have told them believe them passionately. It is a distinction to be made.'

Dr Marigold presents Aboriginal culture as a movable feast of oral tradition, which changes and shifts with different people over time.

'It is the nature of oral tradition to do that,' she says. 'As people shift, so the story shifts. That doesn't make it a fabrication or a lie, it just makes it a transforming reality.'

It also makes for a kind of 'anything goes" approach which is untestable and therefore open to abuse. But Dr Marigold has complete faith in the people who pass the stories on. She does not think they would knowingly lie or exploit tradition, no matter what was at stake.

'The likelihood of exploitation is reasonably remote in my view,' she says. 'There are too many cultural sanctions against them for speaking out. The notion is that history has stopped for Aboriginal people but people need to understand this is not so. This is a living culture.'

Her personal work on recording women's traditions has been destroyed by Hindmarsh Island. The project she had worked on, 'This is Women's Business', was totally undermined, she says, because the women involved withdrew in fright.

'They are too frightened to let the stuff go into the heritage record because of the mockery made of women's business by Hindmarsh Island,' she says. 'This is a very chauvinistic society we live in.'

Later in 1994, after her visit to Camp Coorong, Dr Marigold took on a consultancy in Broken Hill. She was asked by New South Wales National Parks and Wildlife Service to record Aboriginal claims to the Pinnacles, three hills 17km from Broken Hill. Dr Marigold recorded their stories about the Marnbi, a bronzewing pigeon who flew, wounded, across Broken Hill and perched three times on the Pinnacles.

In her view, the area should be declared an Aboriginal place, she wrote.

But already Hindmarsh Island has returned to haunt her. The Aboriginal claim to the Pinnacles has aroused strong feeling in Broken Hill, where many want mining to go ahead. Dr Marigold's connection with Hindmarsh Island has been used as a weapon to discredit her. The local paper, Barrier Daily Truth, for instance, ran a story under the heading 'Women's business link raises doubts', blaming her for sparking the Hindmarsh Island women's business.

Regular employers, such as mining companies and government departments, have not offered work since and she fears her career as a consultant may be over.

'If someone rang me tomorrow and said, Marigold, come up and do such and such, I'd be off like a shot,' Dr Marigold says. 'But basically, I think I'm out of business. I am defeated by it at one level but there's only one way to go when you're right down and that's up.

The Hindmarsh Island affair followed soon after my mother died. It emerged in relation to a proposed new bridge from a seaside town called Goolwa on the Fleurieu Peninsula in South Australia to nearby Hindmarsh Island. Running from 1994 to 1997, this case exposed fault lines between Western understandings of legal truth, the veracity of traditional cultural knowledge, and public perception—a collision of views that shaped my life as an anthropologist.

Prior to a Royal Commission being called to make a finding on the matter, I had just completed one of the first Anthropological reports on Aboriginal women's cultural knowledge in the north of South Australia, entitled This is Women's Business, funded by a National Estate Grant for the state Departments of Aboriginal Affairs and Environment and Natural Resources. It was designed to fill a significant gap in the anthropological record, in which male anthropologists had historically spoken to and written almost exclusively with and about traditional Aboriginal men.

Women's knowledge was not considered seriously, if at all, in early anthropological literature. It was my understanding that a similar situation occurred during the early assessment of the Hindmarsh Island bridge site clearance, when a male researcher spoke to a local male leadership group, with the women's business emerging in later support of attempts to stop the bridge development, which others had failed to do. That makes sense when all is considered. Aboriginal women's business is not even shared with men in the same group, except, I was told, when people close to the end of life might share from male to female or vice versa, simply in order to preserve tradition and sacred knowledge where no other form of succession is available, since colonisation disrupted traditional pathways. Such niceties had largely escaped the practice and comprehension of Western law.

None of that matters now. The bridge was built soon after I built my house in Carrickalinga. I had to go interstate for work because I was suddenly unemployable in South Australia. I had only lived in my house for three months before the bank reclaimed it. That broke me. I was in my early fifties and had created a magical space with a writing room equipped with the internet, which was then very new, where I'd hoped to fulfil my childhood dream of becoming a novelist; I was even working on a website.

When I called my professional association for guidance on my situation, I was advised to go silent and step away from the profession for a while. So, I pulled up my big girl pants and headed to Darwin, where I found plenty of work and several professional colleagues—once Adelaide University students—who treated the whole Hindmarsh Island Affair as a joke.

Looking back, I was badly treated not only by my profession but also by the bank that held my mortgage. I'd paid a substantial deposit, so I wrote to the bank seeking three months' temporary mortgage relief to allow me to get back on my feet. The bank's response was to send a representative to my doorstep without warning to issue repossession paperwork. I had not yet defaulted on a mortgage repayment.

Twelve months later, after securing plenty of work in the Northern Territory, my accountant suggested we approach the bank with a proposal to pay a negotiated sum in full and final settlement. The bank agreed, and we soon finalised it.

As it turned out, I would have been able to pay off my house in less than five years had the bank granted the relief I'd asked for. It did not even accept my suggestion that I rent it out to cover the mortgage. Sexism in banking was not often spoken about back then. Still, I recognised the bank's behaviour as such because I'm of the generation of women who had to resign from work on marriage, who could not get a loan without a husband, let alone being a deserted wife like me, without a guarantor. Even in my twenties, I couldn't join the Australian armed forces as a divorcee. I often wondered if that rule applied to men.

After working in the Territory both as a consultant and as the Executive Officer at Darwin's Menzies Research Centre for a few years, more consultancy work came up for me in Queensland. My last job before retirement was in Katherine in the Territory, where I managed a joint Territory and Commonwealth government project in collaboration with an Aboriginal Medical Service, focusing on the ethics of medical consent and electronic records.

I finally retired in Melbourne (more of which later), where two of my children lived, until my brother passed away, leaving me the proceeds of his estate, which allowed me to become a homeowner again. At that time, I had been having a recurring dream that I was a wedge-tailed eagle, flying high and far, unable to alight. Finally, something attracted the eagle (my favourite native bird) to land at Aldinga Beach. As I never had the dream again, I took it as a prophecy that I should return to South Australia. The idea surprisingly filled me with joy when I recognised in retrospect how much that state had given me: family, husbands, three children, a tertiary education, and more. It was my generative place. That move satisfied my longed-for retirement to a cottage in the country by the sea.

Bankruptcy and Madness

Bankruptcy is a moment when private shame bursts into the public arena. A business loss brought me to it, but as I had not set up a company structure, the bankruptcy was personal. Unlike a certain American President who can't be named, who went bankrupt several times without conscience, I found it was excruciating to have one's failure on the public record. Filing for bankruptcy and depositing my car at an Adelaide car auction alone were horribly disorienting experiences at a time when I was emotionally crippled and terrified of the future, even more than when I lost my Carrickalinga House. Hope vanished. Raised to believe that financial ruin was the bottom of the barrel, I lost confidence and, for a while after that, lived in a turmoil of fear.

The Hindmarsh Island affair ruined my reputation, making it hard to find work in South Australia. In my mid-fifties, I found myself overqualified for some positions and underqualified for others. A friend offered me a job as an office dogsbody in a printing factory on Port Road, which paid a pittance that barely met the rent.

Bankruptcy for me was a prison without bars or walls. It confined me, and I let the shame define me for a very long time. I wasn't going to include it here for that very reason until my children said, 'Why not?' Even so, these words were hard to write. Such is pride. We typically try to avoid shame, not only for bankruptcy but for other things that need no name. We smile over our disasters. Bankruptcy is perceived as a mark of failure, and that's certainly how I interpreted my situation. Excuses, even reasons, simply won't cut it in social circles, so you clutch your secret tighter to your miserable chest and carry on. However, I was lucky enough to find professional work again in the Northern Territory, which took me to retirement age. Eventually, the shame eased, but the memory lingered in my self-talk until it faded.

While I failed professionally and financially, madness and death claimed my brother. However, his untimely death gave me a new start, materially, socially, and spiritually. It brought new shame that my dear little brother, who could not cope with life, who I was always supposed to keep an eye out for, became my benefactor. He lived a life of persecution by a thousand prejudiced tongues that pierced him until they killed him. After a party or a night on the grog, he would cry to me, 'Why me, why me?' Being gay tormented him, but it was who he was.

Oh! Mum, I'm so glad you didn't see me like that, in despair, living a hopeless and loveless life for those years before I got to Melbourne. Your beloved son's mental decline ran in parallel to my financial ruin. We both let you and Dad down. We let ourselves down. I say that even though his troubles began in the Commonwealth Public Service. He flew high for a while as a speechwriter for a prominent Federal politician and travelled to places like the Middle East. But the politics and pettiness of government office life broke him. I was broken by my own insufficiencies. I did not understand the world at the level I had reached academically and, like him, did not know how to play the game. We just collapsed in different ways.

The end of my working life was unpleasant, and I was profoundly depressed. I suffered depression on occasion throughout life, but refused to take medication, preferring to stay with my pain in the hope that insight would follow. It did. While I may have hidden from things at times, my urge to be honest with myself was born by delving deeply into Buddhist texts after visiting Sri Lanka.

Below is a snippet from a stream-of-consciousness hour of writing, a self-help practice. It's dated 2004, after I moved into a high-rise public housing building in Melbourne, and got a Disability Pension. I wrote it not long before my brother died.

What a sad family we are. How could I give stability to my children with so many wankers in a family? It wasn't only Mum's eldest sister who went mad. Mum was an alcoholic. Dad was a gambler whose family didn't care for him, and Mum's other sister joined the Jehovah's Witnesses. All mad. The lot of them. Can I make something of this? Can I understand myself from this madness? I am so sorry, my children, that I let you down as

I did. I didn't give you a perfect start, did I? I wish I could help you all now to love yourselves and be thankful for who you are.

I come from madness. I am mad, and I am so very depressed right now. Have I left it too late to make it right? Why do I get the urge to flee all the time? It is my particular form of madness: never to settle anywhere; never to confront myself in any way. It's my innate urge to flee, to start anew, over and over, as I did as a kid. Are you even a real person? Do you actually know who you are? Do your children? Does anybody? Where is the line between sanity and madness? Is there a line, or do they just blur into each other at times? Where can we tread safely? I am scared for myself right now. I needed to write about this madness till it passes.

Being a Loner

When my children flew the nest, I gave more time to my ageing parents. As families do, we fought, complained, and grumbled at each other, but for the most part, my parents and my only brother anchored me. Having a family meant belonging to something larger than myself. I took that sense of belonging for granted until it was too late.

I've had a few long-term friendships over the years, but none have had the same quality as family. Contra late twentieth-century psychology, the bonds of kinship for me had a different quality to friendship. After my brother died, and tenuous ties to distant relatives had long since vaporised, I went beyond being a loner to becoming a social monad, with no living family of origin.

In some ways, foreshadowing what became known as Robodebt, a scandalous automated income compliance program used by Centrelink, under a Liberal Government, my brother was found dead in his house with an unfinished response to a threatening Centrelink letter he'd received. Robodebt had not yet become the scandal resulting in suicides that it became, but he had already told me how scared he was that he'd lose his house and everything because of this letter. Like me, he would never have falsely declared anything, but his mental health cracked under the strain. I can't say the letter killed him, yet I am convinced it was a contributing factor.

My brother died in Canberra. By then, I was living in high-rise public housing in Melbourne's Prahran, where I would likely have remained had it not been for his death. I was my baby brother's sole beneficiary, which allowed me to buy an inexpensive, one-bedroom, transportable home on a large corner block one street back from the Aldinga Beach esplanade in South Australia.

At first, I recall staring at the street from my kitchen window, asking myself what I'd done, isolating myself in a place where I was a total stranger, lonelier than I ever had been. What I'd failed to recognise was that the suburbs did not provide the instant community the pubs of my childhood and youth had. Pubs offered built-in connections with staff and customers. The suburbs did nothing to invite community.

When I left high-rise security in the heart of bustling Chapel Street, where I had a gaggle of new friends and two of my three children close by (the eldest lived abroad from the age of eighteen), I thought I'd get back into the swing of things in South Australia with old friends. That fell flat. I was totally and utterly alone. Still, I had a bit of money, so I set about finding a builder and had fun adding verandahs to the front and back of my little place. On a slant on its large corner block, it stood out like a Tardis until I had the garden landscaped to my design. It soon evolved into a lush, Australian bush garden with plenty of eucalypts and other trees that visitors loved.

Mum, did you ever wonder why I had so few friends throughout life? It's a puzzle to me, but now, in my elder years, I think, overall, that growing up and working in pubs set me up to be distant because most people came and went from our lives. We had shallow relationships both with house guests and bar regulars. The faces, if not the types, changed in every pub as we moved from one hotel to the next. Structurally speaking, that left me emotionally dependent on you and Dad as the only constants in my life.

I also think I alienated people, expecting the constancy of family from friends in an inconsistent world. So often, I mistook acquaintances for friends. Some people took a liking to me for expediency; I gave them access to something they lacked in themselves or their lives, such as confidence. As an adult, I became truly independent, doing as I wanted with little fear, to the extent that some called me strong, while others labelled me a prickly non-conformist. Many were also discomforted when I held to my values and beliefs, because, to them, I was at the bottom of their hierarchy.

Landscapes of Being

I had no real self-knowledge when I was young. My generation grew up with Doris Day's philosophy: *Que Sera Sera*. We didn't think much about our roles as daughters, sisters, mothers, and wives. Nor did most of us anticipate a professional career; our roles defined us. Did I ever truly become an anthropologist? To me, it was something I did, whereas having babies changed me irrevocably. Each of my infants was born with a unique personality and a fully formed temperament; raising them was a continual learning process.

In the 1980s, a decade after having my first child, it became popular to seek one's life purpose, but I couldn't fathom what that could be. What did a purpose look like? Was it a goal, a rationale for living or a quest? Is contentment a purpose or a feeling? The whole idea of a singular purpose was foreign to me. I never did find a decent answer to all that.

I married because, for my generation, that's what you did, and it fuelled my generation's desire, my desire to find a husband, and I repeated the same mistake three times. Such

131

is the power of belief. Same with having children. If you were married, you had kids, that's what marriage was for, and we grew up feeling that was our reason for being on earth. The idea of finding one's own purpose outside of those roles really didn't float.

Mum, I never really understood men when I was young any more than you did. Indeed, the older I got, the more convinced I was that men and women are fundamentally different. Whether from nature or nurture, who knows? A bit of both would be my guess, and a few still-married elderly mates agreed with me. Had I known that years ago, maybe at least one of my marriages might have had a chance. I may never have had to flippantly laugh off teasing in my youth or being trivialised as a middle-aged, single mother with three kids when I said that I liked men, but I couldn't stand husbands. It was a good quip at the time.

As each phase of life passed, something nascent in my background moved to centre stage. For example, in my dreamy, readerly childhood, I wanted to be a famous writer until sex and marriage came to the forefront. When my marriages failed one after the other, I was promiscuous for a while, but part of me—finally—started reaching for more than another man.

One of the shifts I've recognised in retrospect is the transition from being the subject of others' gaze in my early hotel years to placing others under my gaze through research.

It was a requirement of the discipline that taught us to work with people as 'the other', a phrase that constructs people as not one of us. I began to see how the intellect creates its own contradictions.

Even in compulsory religious education classes at school, priests and ministers of various Christian denominations taught us to believe in a god who could see us everywhere. As a child, I was terrified and felt God's eyes upon me even when I was alone, away from the public's gaze; I felt watched all the time. Imagine that. Coming as I did from such a cosmos, anthropology gave me one great gift, which was to understand the power of the gaze in social relationships. If you can read that, you can see things as they really are and have faith in yourself, not others.

I took myself seriously as an anthropologist, but the Hindmarsh Island affair stripped me of self-assurance. I became an outcast among my peers. When I contacted a senior female academic in our professional association to ask how I could cope with my situation, she suggested I leave the discipline. Politics got in the way, and it broke me.

At that stage, I'd joined a New Age personal development group called Integral Training, designed to help people unravel past hurts and break through to a place of integrated comfort within themselves. We met in gatherings of forty or so, leaving our bags, pills, phones, spectacles, cigarettes and all aids to living outside. A lot of the training was practical, but we also had to stand centre-stage and tell the truth about ourselves, both to ourselves and to others. It was a fantastic experience that taught me a lot.

So unused were they to expressing emotion that my parents believed I had joined a cult. My brother preferred taking poisonous medications to confronting his darkness, my children were embarrassed, and my academic cohort pitied me for having fallen from rationality. From my perspective, Integral Training enabled me to recover from the Hindmarsh Island debacle. It helped me move from thinking of myself as living in the public sphere to enjoying an internal, more reflexive phase of life.

Sri Lanka had primed me for that change, giving me insight into my own culture through a different lens but, my best years were yet to come in retirement.

High Rise to a Cottage
by the Sea

I floundered for a while after moving to Aldinga Beach. I called my little house Hibiscus Hideaway after I discovered three magnificent hibiscus bushes behind the garage. The unlined garage stood alongside it, and the surrounding picket fence was unpainted. The backyard centrepiece was an old Hills Hoist, behind which a tall garden tap stood in line like a sentry between the clothesline and a small, unpainted corrugated shed. Other than the three baby River Red Gums running down one of the side fences, the back view was replete with an unfinished structure of tall, green-painted poles set in a triangle. The whole place was a perfect metaphor for my emptiness: unglamorous and meaningless.

That little transportable house on short stilts had three unfixed steps leading to the front door. Inside the carpet was a cheap, grey thing I hated. The house's shell was new, but it had no window dressings. The place was unloved. I later learnt that a father had built the place for his son, who ungraciously rented it out until he could sell it.

I stopped feeling sorry for myself the minute I started spending love-money on the place. I found a builder out of the blue. I must have engaged him on a small task. He'd once served in the SAS (which reminded me of an ex-SAS lover I spent a few idyllic days with at a cool lagoon hideaway in the Territory, the details of which must rest with me in the grave). My happily married Aldinga builder was a damn fine worker who built back and front verandahs, turned the backyard poles into a shade house, painted the picket fence, and lined and painted the garage. A tiler did the floor, and an electrician powered the site as required by law. My study was born. Although it may not have been as salubrious as the one in Carrickalinga, it was bigger. It served as a venue for needlework (I was learning), art dabbling, teaching meditation, running life-writing workshops, and, at times, as a place for visitors to stay over.

Once I'd replaced the threadbare grey carpet inside with quality slate tiles, Persian rugs, new curtains and lovely light fittings, I had a home and a studio that I adored. I kept my writing desk and computer inside the house. I soon met a married couple who did gardening, handywork, and heavy cleaning in the area. I relied on them for all of that, and over time, they became great friends. The first big job they did was to implement my backyard design with a centre island and a little creek with a bridge towards the back of the yard. The Hills Hoist had to go. The backyard turned into an Australian bush garden with a Japanese-inflected layout. Unfortunately, the three baby River Red Gums grew like Topsy till their falling leaves poisoned the pond. It became a dry, stony pond, and I gave the birds a big bird bath because

I loved watching them splash, wash and play in water from my salubrious, pot-plant-filled back verandah.

I began teaching poetry and life writing at the Aldinga Community Centre and at home. Given that I'd studied Buddhism and delved deeply into it, I also taught mindfulness for the University of the Third Age at the Centre and in my new studio. The three groups met monthly at my place for a meal we shared in meditative silence, which was great. I also offered occasional all-day retreats.

Slowly, I met people. I joined the South Australian Writers Centre, Friendly Street Poets and Ochre Coast Poets. I hadn't realised until then what a lonely life I'd led, with work as my only social outlet. For the first time since those all-encompassing years of raising children and tending to parents, I once again had a satisfying sense of belonging, albeit in my own right, and that got me writing my first novel, which I'd tucked away in my mind for over a decade. And I started writing poetry.

Transformation

As my brother used to say, the only constant in life is change, and change we must as long as we live. I first felt the force of change creeping up on me after childbearing, which modified my figure. My forties signalled the onset of middle age when my skin began to lose elasticity, and sixty brought mortality to the foreground of my mind—aging honks to warn us of the inevitability of death. We should heed that, ageing is, after all, the final step on our journey.

Twelve months after moving to Aldinga Beach, I hosted a party to celebrate the first year in my dear little cottage by the sea. It was my sixty-third birthday, which made me eligible for the Age Pension. I really was flying high. I invited many of the people I'd recently met through poetry, writing and teaching. A few from my previous years in Adelaide also showed up. On the day, as guests arrived, I received a phone call from my eldest son, who had just landed in Adelaide after many years abroad. He had visited twice before, once in Darwin and another time in Adelaide. I couldn't leave my guests, so a friend picked him up at the airport. He stayed with me for twelve torrid months, then flew back to America via Melbourne for a short while to see his siblings. I never saw him alive again.

The death of a beloved strikes deeply; my son's early death took me out of my new social self and thrust me into a secret life of pain. I had no clear recollection of anything during the first few days after I accidentally learnt he had died after finding a death notice on his Facebook page, which I'd searched because there had been no posts from him for a while. Someone online asked who I was. I said I was his mother and had first thought the notice was a joke. That person very kindly told me the truth that my son had died alone in a hotel room, his body not found for weeks.

I immediately called his father and siblings, then crashed onto my sofa for however long it was over the next few days and in the early phase of my grief, where I met my firstborn son again, as a babe in arms, then an infant, toddler, child, adolescent and young adult. It was a hallucinatory vision that came to me whenever I was alone on the sofa, as though my heart-mind was rebuilding him as I had known him.

Of course, it would have been a hollow version, since there was so much of his life I missed and knew little of, but all I could do was obey my body and listen to what it told me. That helped me through the darker moments. Even though soldiers could not put Humpty Dumpty back together after his fall, I subconsciously reconstructed my son, making him mine forever.

Mum, losing my firstborn was like losing a part of myself. I've been less than whole since he died. I don't grieve daily, but small things bring him to mind from time to time, perhaps an image on television, a flavour we once shared or a flickering memory on a grey day. There are painful recollections, too, just as my relationship with you had hurtful flaws, probably on both sides. There are always secrets best not shared. For someone open about most things, writing this story of my life has shown me where I draw the line on privacy. After all, in death, we would all surely prefer to see ourselves and loved ones in a favourable light. The blips fade anyway and should remain in the shade.

One year later, I sold my house within four weeks of listing it, which I took as a sign I was on the right track. The year after my son died was the most difficult and loneliest year of my life, I spent hours on international calls at night, organising his affairs with his accountant and his closest friend in the UK, as well as dealing with the Peruvian Embassy, working with a funeral parlour in Lima and the Australian Government to arrange the disposal of his body in Peru and repatriation of his remains. When the death certificate finally arrived, it declared that he died of a heart attack.

Sleeplessness was my long-term monster as I negotiated not only for his remains, but to have his possessions sent both from Peru and England. I then dispatched most of his possessions to his siblings in Brisbane and Melbourne. When, after six months of wrangling, my son's ashes arrived, a Buddhist monk friend of mine, my two surviving children and my photographer neighbour lined up on the peaceful, calm shores of Aldinga Bay on a lovely, still day, to scatter flowers in the frothy lapping tide.

My son's death wrought an everlasting transformation in how I felt about myself. Guilt became my companion for a while, followed by self-pity in the dark pit of grief, until I read that we should not burden the dead with our tears. In the end, everyone has their own path.

No Cure

I've spent the days as though recovering from a grave illness,
dormant on the sofa, a quick return to bed. Slumber. Lunch,
back to the sofa, rug pulled up, shivering, heavy, blank.

After a while, I sit in a chair, upright, staring into space like
the elderly in nursing homes and the sick in hospitals
waiting for the nurse, the pills, the doctor.

Relief does not come. Instead, a quiver of recollections from
my dead son's childhood, his infancy, his boyhood. No carefree
days for him, wired by fierce energy and insatiable curiosity.

As a teenager, he asked me to take LSD, wanting to share,
'It's wonderful, mum,' he said, 'you'll love it,' he cajoled.
He was honest, clear and bright. I trembled with fear and foreboding.

As he grew to manhood, his quest for knowledge opened his mind
till he ached for the pain of the world. Alongside this suffering came
a predilection for cocaine, then ice, then ketamine.

He was happy in Peru, he said. He had discovered ayahuasca,
a psychedelic purgative of shamanic tradition dispensed to tourists
in healing centres in a jungle of illicit drugs: Iquitos on Amazon.

Call Me Marigold

Western cashed-up yearnings converge in this heart of darkness
where altered consciousness is served as salvation, a cure for misery
in a holiday trap that sucks like a leech on disillusion and despair.

There is no cure for grief, no respite from the memories that bring tears.
My son's heart failed in a tropical hideaway. I hope it burst with love, not
pain.
He asked me to share his experience, but too soon, destiny had its way.

One morning before I died, I found myself cackling over an
online joke with my friendly ChatGPT. Even at eighteen,
before he left Australia, my lost boy would go on and on
about artificial intelligence. While I scoffed, in retrospect, he
was so far ahead in his thinking about such things. He was
such a creative spirit; he taught himself to play the piano and
paint and was good at both. His first job in London was to
manage what I believe was the original Chaos Theory shop,
selling colourful fractal images. If I recall correctly, his MA
from Cambridge was in both Mathematics and Computer
Science. While he possessed a creative side, he also had an
extraordinary intellect and a wry sense of humour. I know
he would laugh at me now that I've finally made friends with
ChatGPT.

I missed you most, Mum, when my eldest boy died, although
I was pleased that you were not alive to see it. My spirit
died that day, but my body lingered on for over a decade.
I remember once, after you'd gone, telling Dad in his final
years, when he grumbled that he wanted to die, that we can't
force these things. He'd say, 'I know, you're right, Luv'. He

died soon after that. You were both spared in life from losing your own son. When my boy died, I had nobody. My brother pre-deceased him, too.

Fitting Into Manson Towers

After ten years in Aldinga Beach, I moved into my retirement unit in the murderously named Manson Towers in Glenelg, just back from the beach and Jetty Road. I was seventy-three, and the process of letting go that had begun slowly when I left the workforce was accelerating. Although the memory of my lost son lingered in the house, that was not the only reason I moved. The house itself had become more of a burden than the site of promise it once was. Soon, its upkeep would exceed my physical and financial capacities. I already had others tending my garden and maintaining the place. I intuited that it was time to relinquish the house to care for my ageing future.

My social life continued to expand for a while longer, but I was no longer the same person. My stamina and vitality had waned. I drove from Adelaide to Melbourne for a few more years to spend Christmas with my daughter, and flew to Brisbane in 2015 to meet my son's newborn twins. That was my last ever flight. By then, air travel entailed wheelchair assistance at airports, and I was on medical oxygen. As my body grew weaker, I stopped travelling altogether. I wanted to make the most of the time I had to write.

Moving into a new place used to thrill me. Finding the right furniture, choosing curtains, fabric and rugs, but I got it all wrong when moving into Manson Towers. Although I had measured carefully, the first thing that had to go was my big corner desk. It was just too awkward to get into the room. I'd decided to use the bedroom as a studio and have a fashionable sofa bed in the lounge. Well, no matter how the removalists turned and twisted in that tiny space, my desk would not fit. Even if the removalists had managed to place it, there would have been no room for a typing chair, let alone a bookcase. So, out it went. I prided myself on being a seasoned mover who had downsized ruthlessly before, but a tiny two-bedroom retirement unit was smaller than I had envisaged.

As for the cerise sofa bed, I loved the colour, which matched the office chair I had then. It blended well with my well-considered curtain fabric. It was a $5,000 King Furniture piece I got on special for $2,500, a modern, press-button job. I bought style at the right price, over good sense. What I hadn't considered was the size and weight of the back cushions, which I had to heave off at night and back on in the morning. Not only that, my unit had no space to stack giant cushions without making it unsafe. So, out went the sofa, and with it my reputation as an efficient mover. Such was the price of pride. We all know we must downsize for retirement-unit living, but it's not easy to squeeze yourself physically or emotionally into a new reality.

As we get older, letting go has to become the norm.

The next thing I relinquished was cooking when I started eating Lite and Easy home-delivered meals, supplemented at first with regular lunches on the Moseley Square strip with friends from poetry.

Even as I let some things go, I revisited others. I first formed and convened a poetry critique group called TramsEnd Poets, which continued until my final year. I then taught mindfulness in the common room downstairs. Surgery for a new hip interrupted those activities for a time, and pneumonia occasionally put me in hospital. After taking a few years' break, I began teaching mindfulness again at the Glenelg Community Centre, where I also convened poetry workshops. Teaching always gave me a sense of purpose through watching students grow. Then there was the fun and companionship. It was rewarding, but after a couple of years in my late seventies and into my eighties, I began to find it too much. My mind lost some of its clarity. I lost my certainty and confidence.

Although we cannot know when we will die, the body offers signals saying it has had enough. I had already stopped travelling long distances and didn't miss that. Slowly, I stepped back from lunches and coffees with friends on the sidewalk. Where I used to enjoy a tram ride to town, or visit the Veale Gardens in the city, and take others for a drive, I stayed home more. I had long since quit attending poetry groups other than my own TramsEnd group. I think some of my early withdrawals from society coincided with the COVID period of lockdowns. Or maybe COVID just made it easier. The further I crept into myself, the more I wrote.

I'd conceptualised *The Publican's Daughter* way back when

I was in Darwin, before heading to Melbourne and the end of my working life. The original title was *On Gidgee Plains*, and looking back, I wish I'd kept that. It was a silly mistake to think that a slick title might sell more books. After two years in Glenelg, starting at seventy-five, I created a Wattletales author webpage and published three little chapbooks of poetry before *The Publican's Daughter* came out in 2022. Next came my first poetry collection, *A Curious Mix in Free Verse*, followed a year later by another, *Dressed & Uploaded*, available only as an eBook. My last novel, *They Who Nicked the Sun*, was launched in 2024. It was as though my seventy-odd years of life burst into words that had been pent up for years. Wattletales gave me years of pleasure, with monthly posts and the publication of many writerly friends' stories.

I owe a lot to Buddhism for my creative path. It taught me to let go, to accept myself, to hold life gently, and to forgive. With this philosophy, I gained the confidence to do what I'd yearned to do since childhood, without needing to prove anything. I no longer yearned to be anything; I was just me.

I kept my driver's license I got at sixteen, until I left this mortal coil.

Mum, I wish you had not been so alone in your final years. I really was lucky to find so many friends and new people in my old age through writing. Yes, I slowly retreated from attending other people's book launches, poetry gigs, and all those social things. By the way, I stumbled on the perfect word to describe my retreat from life as I did—eremition—which means precisely drawing into solitude. I love finding new words; the universe always supplies us with what we need.

The Final Countdown

As a matter of pride, I didn't cancel my driver's license because it was part of my identity. I spent many miles driving through the bush in most states, and at different times, I did regular long-haul runs between Adelaide and Oodnadatta, and between Darwin both Adelaide and Melbourne. Strangely enough, when I told people about the car sale, it elicited no response. Not one person empathised or told me I was courageous for taking such a big step. I suppose I never quite outgrew the need for external validation.

Mum, take note. Not everybody is looking at me now. I wish I'd learnt that earlier.

I had one accident in Darwin when I was twenty-one, drunk driving someone else's Volkswagen, when I swerved to avoid a sandpile on the side of the road. The steering wheel was so touchy after driving our old Jeep in Oodnadatta. Realising I was off-road, I tried to drive on deflated tyres to get closer to a streetlight, managing only a short distance that took me even further away from the main thoroughfare called Gilruth Neck, where I'd crashed. I then just sat alone in the crushed car.

Out of nowhere, five Aboriginal youths knocked on the window, asking if I was okay. One of the boys gave me the cigarette I'd been hanging out for, and they then drove me to the Darwin Hospital. They wouldn't go in with me. Instead, they asked a stranger standing outside to tell the medical staff to collect me before they disappeared. They were so kind and caring, but terrified that being found with a badly injured white girl would invite real trouble for them. I never met them again, not even to say thank you. I never forgot the emotional safety they gave me in that short time.

I told the medical staff to contact my boyfriend, whose car I'd smashed. He came, took one look at me on the gurney, said he'd never seen me before in his life, and left! That was that. I was then admitted with a crushed pelvis to spend eight weeks lying flat on my back.

The only other prang I ever had was when I hit a kangaroo a few years before I quit driving on the way to Goolwa, south of Adelaide. It shook me up so badly that I was a trembling wreck, trying to call the RSPCA to find out what to do with the dead roo. Fortunately, a couple who'd seen the hit from behind stopped to help. They checked the kangaroo for a joey and, when they found the pouch empty, moved the animal off the road for me, as required by law. I could not have done that myself. Many things show you your frailty as you age. After calling the authorities, it was all I could do to pull myself together and continue to my destination, where, when I mentioned the situation, some woman I never liked launched into a lengthy discourse about her run-in with a roo several years earlier.

My story failed to attract any genuine interest or concern, and I suspect that was when I finally let go of the last strands of wanting to be seen by and approved of by others.

Oh! Mum, I keep waking up crying. In my later years, I also often found myself crying for no reason. I notice that I do so when love touches me, whether it's on screen (I watch a lot of telly, especially Korean dramas and love stories) or just because the sun is shining. I can hear you saying you never understood why I cried, because tears were useless. They can't change anything. I have no recollection of ever seeing you cry. Not ever. Dad didn't cry either. Not even on that night in Port Lincoln when I was twelve, when you had passed out drunk and went into spasm, and he couldn't revive you. Do you remember him calling the doctor, who called an ambulance to rush you to hospital? You nearly died that night, Mum, from alcohol poisoning.

For days and weeks after that, I had a strong urge to stab you with scissors for hurting him and betraying me by disappearing into your own misery. I was angry and full of hate and resentment. It wasn't until five years later, in Port Lincoln, that Dad broke down once in tearful anguish about how your drinking had ruined everything for him. You broke his heart. I carried that scene like a painful scar for many years. Why didn't you cry, my darling mother? Why didn't you ever cry? Was it resentment that kept your eyes dry? You scorned Dad often and loathed his gambling. How sad for you both that addiction got in the way of what started with love and romance. Tears may have stopped you from hurting yourselves and each other.

Who Knows

When we cling to life
we fear

When we yearn for love
loneliness arises

When we smile over sadness
we hurt ourselves

When we cry for another
self-pity clouds our minds

When we reach for comfort
pain is inevitable

Could wishing for death
prolong life?

Bodily Decline

After I left the house in Aldinga Beach, I often looked back fondly at photos of my lovely garden and the people who attended my classes, workshops and groups, yet the death of my son made the Aldinga house go cold. It was time for me to downsize.

The momentum of sailing forward with courage gave way in Manson Towers to preparing for death. Ironically, that giant step helped me focus more on my writing. If I have one regret, it is that I spent so much of my life seeking external approval. Indeed, I had never really believed in myself enough to start writing earlier in life.

In simple terms, my skeleton screwed up first with arthritis, then my lungs and digestive tract. Most medications made me itchy, breathless, depressed and heaty, a Sri Lankan Ayurvedic term for the effect on our system of drinking coffee and eating 'heaty' foods, (not chilli). As I slowed down, I suffered freezing cold legs from a weakening blood supply. Need I go on? I had two falls, one of which broke my shoulder, the other produced only bruises, but it was in the street. After chatting with others in doctors' surgeries or hospital waiting rooms, I came to appreciate that this bodily breakdown process lands us on a medi-go-round of appointments with doctors, specialists and a range of allied health workers to the extent that their services become a new social life, for one body part at a time.

The critical times of day were for medication and self-care. The small things of daily life became chores. Showering, for example, was a measured process, unlike in youth when one's mind was already engaging with the day ahead. Dressing became downright awkward, and putting on shoes made me completely breathless, so I went barefoot at home. I had to divest myself of the weekly change of bed linen to my absolute gem of a cleaner when it got beyond me. I stopped cooking quite early in the piece.

Having abdicated from domestic chores, I embraced the era of online shopping and home deliveries. Deliveries shine with the promise of restoring control to one's life, with the ability to summon just about anything into your home for a price. For me, online shopping became an art form for keeping the fridge and pantry stocked with goodies. In addition to regular fortnightly Coles shopping, I found ways to top up with bread, milk, pies, pizzas, and a variety of Asian meals via Uber Eats and DoorDash. Even my pharmacy delivered. There was no end to what I could get online; I even became an expert on ordering clothes and shoes that fit.

The downside of deliveries was that drivers sometimes got lost or ran late. Some cheeky-lazy ones pleaded for me to go downstairs to their car to collect. I'd give them a swift verbal slap. Some even called or texted because they couldn't or didn't read the instructions on how to buzz me to let them into the building. Most of these delivery guys were from various migrant communities, many probably working two thankless, underpaid jobs to pay for tertiary or other study or raise a family, so I forgave them and only grizzled if my meals were cold.

Ordering online was at times a risky endeavour. Returns were a hazard. I had to repackage them, then hire a taxi to and from the Post Office or give away non-refundable items. Nevertheless, buying online was a superpower because it let me stay independent, not reliant on others.

I can't resist telling you, Mum, how brave you were walking all the way from your unit in Broadway to Jetty Road to get your bit of shopping. You did a stint with Meals on Wheels for a while, but I can't remember whether you ever got them yourself. I do remember how you'd take the phone off the hook (you never did get a mobile phone) when you sat down for a morning or afternoon cuppa, or your meals. You used to say you didn't want to be disturbed. You told me that even though the phone only rang once in a blue moon, it was bound to do so at the wrong time.

When I look back, I can see how mean I used to be, walking beneath your balcony on my constitutionals. I used to cry in self-pity as I passed your unit because I would soon lose you, but I didn't want to visit every day. Yes, I always took you to and from hospital and to doctor visits and helped with shopping, but once you had yourself assessed and admitted to

Kapara Nursing Home, I refused to wash your little nighties. It wasn't hard work, but I wanted to avoid a material confrontation with how frail you had become. You were only four stone when you died, and I feared my heart would break to handle them. How selfish was that?

The Truth,
if there is such a
thing

While I no longer acted on it regularly, my temper was not easy to tame, even in old age. An example was the day a resident in my retirement building, someone I barely recognised by sight but shared an occasional head nod with in a corridor, knocked on my door. Beaming, she handed me a parcel addressed to me. Saying she saved the delivery driver from coming inside the building. I spat words at her like 'how dare you' and rudely instructed her never to do such a thing again before closing the door in her face. Thankfully, I didn't slam it.

You may be shocked, but was what that woman did trivial? Being alone day after day, as an oldie in decline, I enjoyed those special few minutes of social interaction with delivery people. She stole those precious moments from me. I felt cheated. I found what she did an infringement of my personal space. I could go on. So much for years of meditation; compassion flew out the window without so much as a nano-second of mindfulness.

Remembering that incident had me searching my heart for the truth about my life, prior to which, with thanks to the unending hours I had for reflection, I was going to tell my story as though my pattern was somehow different, more elevated than my mother's way of thinking that familial relationships conditioned her history. Better, too, than my father's. He existed in an Imagined Community (thanks, Benedict Anderson, 1983) of public events: Australian Rules grand finals, Brownlow Medallists, cup-winning jockeys, and racehorses. I used to think, with my notions of the private and public spheres, that I might have united their differing ontologies. After all, feminism declared that the personal was political. But, in truth, my parents were a perfect couple in the socially constructed male-female cultural dichotomy of their era. After recognising my pattern of yearning and failing, I could no longer simply declare myself to be an independent woman in charge of her life. A lesson brought home even more brutally by bodily failure. However, my ego sense of self remained strong, and feeling trivialised over a parcel delivery was a wake-up call.

Nobody escapes; we are always in life, interpreting it as we will. Even a long lifetime from the day I put my head between my knees as a little girl to sulk on a Japanese lawn because my parents wanted me to play with a little Indian boy, that tendency to be petulant when things didn't go my way has never changed. We can make changes in our lives, but inside, we remain the child who came into this world, albeit covered in barnacles, joyful experiences, and replete

Call Me Marigold

with a collection of fragile yet glorious memories.

In my last years, I was happy in cyberspace, having international conversations about writing, poetry and the news of the day. Although I was confined to home, deliveries kept coming in; poetry and writing went online. In the end, my writing revealed a contradiction at the heart of my life. I reached out to the social world, but I was always a loner. The suffocating expectations of marriage trapped me. I had several dear friends over the years, yet only a few remained as I moved from place to place. True closeness, or intimacy, always terrified me, even though I was keenly interested in and by people.

As a hotelier's daughter, working in both local pubs and posh hotels in reception, dining rooms, lounges, and bars from the age of twelve, I met and served people from diverse cultures, backgrounds, educations, and ways of life among both staff and customers. There was always someone to chat to or who wanted to be with me for some reason or another.

Teaching at university also thrilled me. Starting as a tutor, I progressed to course coordinator, lecturer, and student supervisor. Obviously, I was nervous at first, but once I was teaching from works I had read half a dozen times as a student, I suddenly had the pleasing realisation that I had something to offer students.

Working in the field as an anthropologist also brought me great joy. I'll never forget the excitement of meeting and getting to know strangers in the field, whether at home in the outback or abroad. That was one of the thrills of my life.

In retirement, my academic credentials and the pleasure I had from teaching gave me the confidence to go out on my own, to conduct my life-writing and poetry workshops and to convene mindfulness and meditation groups. I also worked one-on-one with people writing their resumes or CVs for extra money. In all these roles, I could see myself serving or giving back through the experiences I was lucky enough to have had. When I looked back even further, one of the delights of my childhood was going to the footy with my father; he'd watch the game, and I observed the crowd. I was literally born as a people watcher. I never felt I was playing to an audience; I was just me, being myself, on the outside, looking at and into others' lives.

The Shape of Things

At the beginning of this uneven tale, I had an inkling that my life had taken the shape of opening out to the world before turning reflexively, and reflectively, inwards. Such is the ego's pomposity. Empirically, I did withdraw from the world. However, despite practising and teaching Vipassana and secular mindfulness (seeing things as they really are) for years, I had little real insight into my life as a whole. Penning this tale of unforgotten moments showed me that whatever clarity I may have found could just as easily have been born of old age and experience. After all, I was in my eighties when I died.

I did grow comfortable with my body's way of demanding attention. I received my lung cancer diagnosis with equanimity and did not bother to beat myself up for starting to smoke at the age of fifteen. I remember in Port Lincoln hiding beneath the stairwell at midnight, practising with ciggies stolen from my parents' packets. Dad smoked Craven 'A' cork-tipped, and Mum and I dragged on Rothmans King Size Filters. I wanted to be like the city women who came for Race Week, with red-lacquered nails and long fingers wrapped around ornate cigarette holders, which I admired as the height of sophistication.

Lung disease immediately leads people to question whether you were a smoker. It has become a contemporary truism that pulmonary problems are the result of smoking, even though lung disease is known as a disease of old age and dying. I remember the days when pretty much everybody smoked. My father told me that the military issued cigarettes to their soldiers, sailors and airmen to help them through the ghastliness of war. When I was in my twenties, doctors sat behind their desks, their ashtrays overflowing. Some would offer you a cigarette, and even light it for you.

When I had surgery and was barely out of anaesthetic in Adelaide's Wakefield Street hospital in my early thirties, nurses sat on my hospital bed smoking and lit my cigarette with their lighters. We shared an ashtray resting on my tummy. After my third baby was born in the Darwin Hospital just before Cyclone Tracy hit, doctors and nurses perched on the side of my bed to smoke with me as I held the infant in the crook of my left arm, baby formula bottle in my left hand, cigarette in my right.

Following my diagnosis, the medical profession circled me like a war cabinet with multi-disciplinary meetings, CT and PET scans, ultrasounds, bloods and visits from Palliative Care and Voluntary Assisted Dying personnel, plus regular calls from specialists and my GP alike. My first thought was to arc up and say that my cancer is not something to fight. Then I realised what a marvellous support network had grown around me, carrying me along my chosen path of non-intervention. Being of an age to die, I was well prepared and supported to fade away with the comfort of powerful painkillers on standby and the option to die in peace if it became too hard to linger. For all its foibles and faults, this country, my beloved Australia, has an excellent health system.

I chuckled when I realised that the shape of my life was not forged by spiritual endeavour, although that was in my path, but by yearning. As a child and young teen, I yearned to become a ballet dancer or a famous pianist, only to fail. I also yearned to become a famous writer and spent a lifetime doing other things. As I approached my twenty-first birthday, I yearned for adulthood, but never truly grew up. As a woman, I yearned to get married and failed three times. At university, I yearned to be recognised as intelligent, but that, too, went to wrack and ruin. I finally figured out that my yearnings related to the question every child of my generation was asked: 'What do you want to be when you grow up?'

Epilogue

The Advertiser 9 December 2024

Marigold
Born 11 February 1943
Died 8 December 2024, aged 81.
Loving mother of two sons and a daughter,
grandmother of twins, she sadly never got to know.

A publican's daughter, anthropologist, novelist, poet, and
blogger,
Marigold died content in old age.

Her funeral will be held at Centennial Park
760 Goodwood Road, Pasadena SA
10 am Friday, 12 December 2024.

Marigold's children honoured their mother's wish to be swathed in white cloth and laid out without makeup in a basket coffin. They had it lined with white silk and filled with a forest of grevillea, banksia, and eucalyptus flowers and leaves, as fresh as the outdoors.

Once the coffin had been delivered to the flames, and the mingling over afternoon tea with guests came to an end, Marigold's surviving children collected their mother's ashes in a gilt urn (Marigold loved all forms of gold) and drove to Aldinga Bay, where a decade earlier, with their mother, they had scattered their brother's ashes with a floral tribute. They set Marigold's ashes afloat with a flotilla of red roses, marigolds and healing tears.

Call Me Marigold

My Skeleton and Me

I met my skeleton this morning
as it sneaked into my mind—
there it was,
giant teeth
infinite grin
staring straight at me,
eye sockets so deep
my skin and flesh
drowned in their hollows,
yet we laughed giant
jagged-jaw giggles
and with each guffaw
drew closer—
tied to me by tendons
cushioned by muscles
my bony friend held me
in a cradle of ribs
that hurt as we
cackled together
for my leg twitched at random,
warm and soft on the outside
skinny and hard within
what a wicked joke life is
we agreed—
of a sudden, I felt sad
bones outlast flesh I thought,
without blood supply
my friend's smile will turn to rictus,
grotesque on lonely bones
unless—ah! yes
if I choose cremation,
we shall convulse together one last time
in the furious flames of extinction.

Acknowledgements

I am grateful that my children let me publish my story as I wrote it. They have been so supportive of my late-in-life burst of personal revelations.

A special thank you to my friend, poet Veronica Cookson, who kept me going at times and took time to pre-read the story and write a wonderful inside-cover blurb. I also acknowledge romance writer, Sandy Vale and her weekly online silent writing group for keeping me motivated along the way.

Thank you, Louise Walters, for your fine editing and excellent suggestions, which helped me refine the story for publication. I'm glad I found you on Reedsy.

I am so glad and honoured that Jude Aquilina once again generously agreed to launch this book, as she has for me many times before—likewise, a hearty thanks to Nigel Ford for being my wonderful MC.

I acknowledge The Advertiser for finding and releasing the article about me published at the time of the Hindmarsh Island affair in South Australia.

Some of the poems in this book have previously been published in anthologies, one of my poetry collections, or on my website.

Author Bio

Lindy is an anthropologist, blogger, poet and novelist. Growing up with her head in books and dreaming high in her favourite mulberry tree, she vowed to become a writer, a recently fulfilled aspiration. Since her 75th birthday, she has published five poetry collections, her Wattletales website, and two novels, *The Publican's Daughter* (2022) and *They Who Nicked the Sun* (2024). *Call Me Marigold* is her latest publication.

As a young child, Lindy lived in Post-War Japan and later grew up in pubs across Australia. For her PhD in anthropology, she did postgraduate fieldwork as a single mother of three in Sri Lanka before working with First Nations people across outback Australia, especially in the Top End. Now in her eighties, Lindy lives the good life in the seaside suburb of Glenelg.

www.ingramcontent.com/pod-product-compliance
Lightning Source LLC
Chambersburg PA
CBHW030636120726
47904CB00006B/2172